A BONA FIDE HUSBAND
HUSBAND
and other stories

A Paperback Original
First published 1991 by
Poolbeg Press Ltd,
Knocksedan House,
Swords, Co. Dublin, Ireland.

© 1991 Lilian Roberts Finlay
Poolbeg Press receives financial assistance from The
Arts Council / An Chomhairle Ealaíon, Ireland

ISBN 1 85371 107 1

Cover design by Ciara Davis
Typeset by Typeform Ltd
Printed by The Guernsey Press,
Vale, Guernsey, Channel Islands.

A BONA FIDE HUSBAND

and other stories

Lilian Roberts Finlay

POOLBEG

For Antony Farrell
With gratitude for his friendship

Contents

In the Beginning

The honeymoon was over. Tom had gone back to work. The new life had begun.

Eily snuggled down deeper into their brand-new double bed. She knew very well why she was not jumping out of bed, and facing this New Life. The honeymoon is over, Tom had said last night, back to the Job in the morning. His enthusiasm was unmistakable.

Eily had experienced a sense of disillusion that a honeymoon could not go on for a lifetime. She was awaiting more out of the week of honeymoon; more of joy, less of pain. There was a dim feeling of disappointment in the honeymoon but perhaps it was disloyal to feel like that.

In bed last night, Eily had begun to explain to Tom how saying the honeymoon is over was like giving no one a second chance. Tom was sleepy, and Eily would learn that "debating in bed was not one of his habits." He always used the identical phrase for the identical need, and "not one of his habits" was a favourite. In the middle of her struggle to communicate her feeling about honeymoons, without revealing her sense of disappointment, he yawned loudly.

"Tell you what," he mumbled, "we'll go over and

see Mam and the family after tea tomorrow, tell them about London, and the air-raid shelters going up in Hyde Park... they won't believe a word of it..."

And then this morning, he was the one to rise promptly, full of high spirits, insisting that she stay in bed, bringing her a cup of tea. He was fussy and concerned about the sit of his tie and the contents of his brief-case. Laughingly feigning dramatic passion, he kissed her goodbye, then ruined it all by shouting back from the hall door, "Don't forget we are going over to Mam's tonight!"

Eily drew the eiderdown up to her chin. She would not begin the new life on a day that was going to end with a visit to Tom's mother. That visit could easily be postponed for a week, or a month. Or a year as far as Eily was concerned.

On this first day, she wanted to anticipate Tom's home-coming as the prelude to a long cosy evening of lingering over the meal, of talking heart-to-heart for endless hours. This very first night of the new life in their own home must be a night of total intimacy. Yes, Eily dreamed, a first night—if last night had to be the last night of the honeymoon, then tonight would be the romantic scene Eily loved, perhaps making love on the fireside rug with only the firelight for a lantern. But would Tom be likely to make love on the rug in front of the fire? She could imagine him saying another of his favourites, "A time and a place for everything" and, at the proper moment, marching her across the hall into the bedroom.

To quell the slight feeling of disloyalty, Eily defended him to herself. Tom might be self-conscious, this gave him a sense of his own dignity.

Also he accorded dignity to others, which maybe was why he was so popular. Eily smiled when she reflected how popular Tom was; he had so many friends. She felt she had won a prize in Tom. Her faint disappointment merely marked her as lacking in appreciation. If only he had not said that the honeymoon was over, so jubilantly, failing to understand that she thought the honeymoon should be just beginning and that each moment of this present time would be spent in a secret exploration of its as-yet-unfulfilled delights.

But tonight Tom had to visit his mother. The thought brought her back to the proposed evening visit with a surge of such distaste that she leaped from the bed, and fled through the kitchen into the garden.

Eily loved the garden. Because of the garden, she had cajoled Tom into renting the cottage. He considered it too far from town but the rent was low. The front of the cottage gave onto a quiet road, the back and sides were all greenery. There was a hundred years of unplanned planting gone into this garden. Flowering trees were mixed in with apple trees; there were roses everywhere. Someone had made quaint garden seats with odds and ends of wood, all worn now and in need of a coat of paint, but comfortable and placed to catch the sun.

Eily sat down and tucked her feet under her. No one, she thought, could feel unhappy in this old garden. Tom had grumbled about all the work to be done in a big garden. He had, in fact, referred to the garden as a bit of a wilderness. But she would help him, and after all, what else was there to do with all the time they would have for spending together.

Eily's eyes were closed luxuriously against the sun...she pictured Tom digging and planting while she gathered great baskets of apples for all the apple-pies she would bake for him. Adam and Eve in Eden, never banished—living there for ever and ever.

Eily heard the side-gate click. Before she could move, a little boy came running around the path. He had a kitten clutched into his jersey.

"Mammy said would you like a cat?"

Eily took the white kitten. Too small to purr, it nestled contentedly against her flimsy nightdress.

"What's your name?" she asked the little boy.

"It's Francis, but me daddy calls me Franko."

"Franko is nice," smiled Eily, "it's different."

"And will you take the cat?" asked Franko pleadingly, "I mean the kitten. Our cat has six, and Mammy can only get homes for two...please take it...Mammy says if they don't get homes, she will have to send them to America and then we will never see them again. Please, will you? Mammy says Fuzz has too many too often but that's not her fault only thirty a year is more people than Mammy knows to ask...will you?"

Eily stroked the little kitten. "Are all the kittens white?"

"That is the only white one. Mammy said you would like a white one because you are, because you are..." He had forgotten what his Mammy said.

"Because I am new?" Eily offered.

"Something like that," he was relieved, "there's another one, blacky-whitey and two all black."

"Do you think your Mammy would give me the blacky-whitey one as well?" Eily asked.

His eyes opened wide, "Do you mean you'd take two?"

"Why not," Eily smiled at his wonder, "I am sure Tom, my husband, loves kittens."

"Come with me, so!" shouted the little boy, not noticing that Eily was wearing a nightdress.

Eily had him point out his house and she promised to follow in a few minutes.

Eily enjoyed talking with Franko's Mammy. She and her husband, whose families had lived for generations in this area, had a market garden.

With the other kitten, instantly named "Clogs" for his four white feet, Eily was given a cabbage and a little bag of tomatoes. She felt very pleased and proud and immeasurably more mature. All shadowy doubt dispersed, the new life was beginning beautifully...nice neighbours, two adorable kittens, and a cabbage for Tom's dinner.

Eily had never cooked a cabbage but she had a wedding present of a huge cookery book and lots of brand-new pots and tins. There were some apples on the cottage trees quite big enough to pick. Why not a scrumptious apple-pie to start the new life? Eily counted her money. Now she wished she had not spent all her savings in London but things in the big stores there had looked so glamorous and almost for nothing—but four hats? Eily loved hats and there would be years to wear them. She made a list with the help of the cookery book: six potatoes, six slices of cooked corn-beef, four ounces of margarine, six ounces of flour, some sugar, some bread-soda for the cabbage (the book said "a pinch" but could one buy a pinch)—Eily wished she had taken Domestic Economy in school instead of French but then Sister

Theresa had said only duds took cookery, so it must be easy. Yesterday, Tom had thought of stocking up with bread and tea and butter and milk, and even marmalade—this last a stroke of genius in Eily's eyes. Imagine remembering marmalade!

Eily made a place for the kittens in the shed, and took out her bicycle. Franko's Mammy had told her that the village was known as "The Cross," a few small shops and a Church, at a cross-roads. Eily was smiling to herself as she cycled along. She knew very well that anything more important than "The Cross" would intimidate a first-time housekeeper like herself.

Eily's parents were dead since she was a small child. All her years of growing up were passed in a boarding-school, and since then as a filing-clerk in a busy office in the town. Living in lodgings, she had shared (with other girls like herself) the slap-dash attentions of the landlady, Mrs Stakelum. This lady's pride, and claim to fame, was the great girth of her bosom which she was careful not to diminish by an over-indulgence in active domestic chores. The girls found her comforting and kind. They accepted the bosom and forgave her other inadequacies. Four years of Mrs Stakelum's "digs" had left Eily with a very sketchy idea of regular well-cooked meals, and a very easy-going attitude to household routine.

Tom was not too impressed with "Snowhite" and "Clogs." And, Eily thought, he was even less impressed with her cooking. The cabbage was stalky, the pastry was like cardboard, and his share of the corn-beef disappeared in one bite. He praised the new neighbour's tomatoes, making two sandwiches of them which he polished off with a cup of tea.

Tom, Eily was to learn, could at times be lavish with praise if the results were worth it. He saw no need for reassurance for efforts made. That would be "talk for talk's sake"—a motto of his with useful variations. His main concern this evening was to get going over to his Mam's.

So Eily hurried. She had piled the dishes in a basin. She was putting on her coat.

"Surely you are going to wash these things?" Tom queried. She smiled at him, "Sure I'll have nothing to do tomorrow when you are gone to work!"

Tom was aghast. "Every day brings its own work," he said sternly, "and no one leaves dirty dishes overnight. You had better do them now. Tomorrow is another day."

Taking off her coat, Eily thought of something Mrs Stakelum used to say each evening, as she took pride of place among the girls gathered around her kitchen after tea, "A good fire and enough to eat is half feeding!" Eily never knew exactly what it meant but it seemed very well-intentioned. It was fine for Mrs Stakelum, and Tom, to have all these sayings for her betterment—it was like living in a Vere Foster Headline Copy, the one in which she had first learned to write. She never could remember the ends of these lines—wasn't there one about "Woman's work?" There's another disloyal feeling, thought Eily, glimpsing Tom in the little parlour. He was stretched out on the couch with a newspaper. There are more ways of beginning a new life than sharing it.

Tom's father greeted them at the door. He had a completely different type of personality from Tom's mother. Eily thought he was out of a different class, a different age and maybe a different world. He was big and grizzled and rumpled. He enfolded Eily in a bear-hug lasting a little too long for comfort and he held her firmly against him as he asked her non-stop questions about her health and her happiness. Leaving no time for answers, he disappeared up the stairs. Eily gazed after him, she rather liked the nuzzling warmth of him—when it was over.

Tom said dismissively, "He's doing door-porter tonight. You haven't forgotten Mam's at-home night—this is Friday!"

In the dining-room, a family crowd had gathered around the table for the Friday night game of cards. There were the two married daughters and their husbands, the younger son and his girl-friend, the widower from next door, a neighbour and his wife. On the table, glasses and bottles and ash-trays gave an air of conviviality.

Tom's mother was seated at the top of the table near the fire. In studied deliberation, she removed her concentrated gaze from her hand of cards, giving the newcomers a surprised acknowledgement.

"We were not expecting you," she said shortly. "Batt and the wife have joined us. Twelve would be rather too many."

If Tom found anything wrong with this strange welcome, he gave no sign.

"We are just back from our honeymoon," he said loudly and jovially, "I'm sure you are all dying to hear all about it!"

"Absolutely dying!" chortled a brother-in-law, "All!" The younger brother's girl-friend giggled. Eily was painfully aware of many pairs of eyes fixed on her face. Tom put an arm around her shoulder lightly. She felt he was quite at home, this atmosphere was his natural element.

"Did you know," began Tim, "that the English are building air-raid shelters under Hyde Park? It's serious, you know. We had a strange..." But this was too much for the brother-in-law.

"Strange?" he shouted, "Begin at the beginning. First night! Scene One!"

Through the guffaws that followed this hilarious innuendo, Eily heard Tom's mother banging the table with her heavy rings. Her voice pierced the cigarette haze, "We will return to the cards, if you please. Tom can get something to do until the second game. Maybe the supper. Good practice for the new wife."

Eily turned away from the card-players. Tom was rummaging on the side-board. He was examining the envelopes on a letter-rack. To her surprise, he opened and read all the correspondence, some bank statements, and electricity bills.

"They are not yours!" Eily whispered agitatedly.

Tom looked amused. "Course they are," he said, "I always read them." He opened a few drawers in case he had missed anything. He smiled fondly, "The same old junk! Come out to the kitchen."

There were plates of sandwiches neatly ranged beside the second-best tea-cups and saucers. Tom helped himself to a sandwich, and then to another sandwich.

"Have one," he offered. Eily demurred; she felt sure the sandwiches were counted. "I'm not hungry, maybe we could just tip-toe out and leave them to their cards?" She was almost begging.

"And miss the supper! Are you mad! No, we'll

join the second game. We'll get the last bus easily. Stop worrying! You put the kettle on—put the gas low. I'll carry in the trays. I can put them on the side-table. They must be nearly ready soon."

If Eily had remembered about the card-game, and the at-home night, she thought she would have refused to come. It would have taken a bit of courage; Tom could be so adamant. His family were all card-mad experts, and she was not. There would be the usual inquest after the second game. Tom's mother would not hesitate to call Eily "a little silly," "a little dreamer," in a voice that clearly said "dunderhead," "stupid fool," "imbecile." Eily could not, and never would, understand how people remembered what cards had "gone before." Sometimes she forgot which suit was trumps or even if it was a no-trump game. In school, the only card-game was "Happy Families" but she did not care to excuse herself to Tom's mother with so paltry an excuse...best, really, to try harder to please.

Tom's mother made a big effort to be pleasant during the supper, detaching her mind from the first rubber to ask Eily a question or two.

"And how is the cooking coming along?"

"Aha!" laughed Tom, "Eily made an apple-pie today."

"An apple-pie bed?" put in the brother-in-law quickly.

The neighbour's wife choked and spluttered and was soundly thumped on the back by her husband.

"The price of a stone of flour is disgraceful in an agricultural country," enunciated Tom's mother from the top of the table.

The stone of flour! Eily now remembered the little

grocer's surprised face when she had asked for six ounces of flour and four ounces of margarine. "I am new here," she had smiled at him, "we have the cottage with the mimosa tree." So one should buy flour by the stone? The little grocer had measured out the flour into a paper-twist, and cut a small piece of margarine in half. "Will there be anything else, Missus?" he had responded gallantly and Eily knew her face went pink from the unaccustomed "missus." And of course, six ounces of flour had not left any flour over for rolling out the pastry which, presumably, was the reason it was so tacky. Eily wondered at herself...how a girl who had earned her own living in an office could be such a ninny...mooning over kittens and not knowing how to buy flour.

Eily had plenty of time to think her own thoughts. It had been decided that there was no place for her in the second game. She sat in a corner with a newspaper. It was cold so far from the fire, she would have liked to get her coat but that would look rude. Also there was a danger of meeting Tom's father out in the hall. It wasn't that she disliked him: it was that it was odd the way no one ever mentioned him.

Eily was allowed to wash up the supper dishes. She was instructed to take extreme care of the good ware.

Going home in the bus, Tom was in a state of elation. The brother-in-law had told him, he said, that they were expecting him back at the club for the championships, and Mam had said that he could have lunch there with her on Saturdays to save him from trekking out to the cottage and, as Mam and he agreed, wasting time when he could be knocking a ball around.

"It's bad enough," said Tom, "to have to work half-days on Saturdays. The bigwigs don't go in on Saturday—it should be done away with: no one ever does a stroke on a Saturday. I'll go straight to Mam's from the office, and I'll probably have a few 'jars' with the lads after the game. I should be back in the cottage about nine or it could be a bit later if we are playing away, and then..."

Eily was not listening. The dim disappointment of the morning had returned. Its edges were sharper now and threatened to cut into the fabric of her life. She struggled with a thought too difficult to come clear. Was marriage for two people or only for a woman? The two people entering into the holy bond of matrimony, did that not set them apart? Both of them or only the woman? Did the man lay himself open to ribaldry, exposing himself for the gratification of fun-makers? Vaguely Eily had thought of marriage as a sacred place, a secret cell into which two people walked hand-in-hand. No one else ever came there, no one knocked on the door. If Tom was totally unaware of this lovely, solemn cell, then she must be in there by herself. She wondered if marriage could be a trap with steel teeth, ready to snap on her.

"So that's all settled then?" Tom was saying as he tucked his arm through hers, to walk up from the bus-stop to the cottage. Eily liked the warm feel of his arm, it was comforting. Did his arm feel her heart beating? She looked up at him. Tom was so handsome, even when he yawned, as he did now, "Our last long lie-in tomorrow! It's a good job I had

14

this Saturday off! Saturdays after this are going to be murder!" His voice was younger than she had noticed before, teasing, tempting, "You will have to do without me on a Friday night in future!"

"Won't you be coming home?" Eily asked.

"Oh sure!" Tom replied very airily, "but only for my dinner and a sound sleep—and not for any hanky-panky, mind! Not on a Friday night!"

Eily remembered that at their wedding service the old priest had given a little talk about four things to have in a good marriage. A sense of humour was one of them. Did that mean you had to smile when you felt affronted? She did not smile.

Tom was first into the bedroom, and into bed.

"Hurry up!" he called to her, "it's lovely in here!"

"Coming," she replied. Now she was in no hurry. She brought in the kittens to give them milk; she was stroking them and whispering to them, hesitating about putting them back out in the shed. They were part of an earlier, carefree mood...

"Eily!" There was no doubt he was getting impatient.

She had left her nightdress in the bathroom cupboard when she was hurrying out to Franko and his Mammy early that morning. It seemed a long time since morning, almost as if a lot of her life had slipped by today. She undressed slowly and put on the wedding nightdress. In the mirror, she looked the very same as always. Not desolate. Not abandoned.

"Eily!"

In the bedroom, she stood looking at Tom in bed. She had a question to ask him, but should she?

"Eily, you certainly know how to get a fellow

worked up. Come on, what's keeping you?"

The question trembled on her tongue: what about the garden on Saturdays?

"Tom..." but how not to spoil his pleasure in his Saturday sport?

"Eily, you look gorgeous! Will you come into bed before I have to get out and drag you in!" His handsome features were set in a look of pleading adoration.

To Eily, Tom was irresistible. With the strange feeling of passing by a milestone in her life, she let the question fall. It would never be asked; and if it had, Eily was to learn that it would never have been answered.

The Woolwich Tunnel

As anyone would be, who receives a phone-call from a forgotten voice after a silence of thirty-five years, Lucy was completely taken aback. With prior warning, she would have thought up an excuse. Quite often, Lucy made excuses to refuse invitations which might disturb the even routine of her day. After a lifetime of busy family life, she had adapted herself to being a widow and to living alone. Five years ago, it had not been easy to adapt. There were months of feverish activity, of trying to fill every evening with a pleasurable outing. There was a winter of joining night-classes to learn skills in which she had very little interest. There had been sudden decisions to get the car out on the highway and cross the city to visit a married son whose wife soon made it clear, gently enough, that unexpected callers were not always welcome. The longing for a constant, familiar presence was hard to banish. Gradually it had come to Lucy that if she had not a person who belonged to her alone, to enquire if she were sick or well, to pay a little compliment on the new dress or the new hair style, then there was no reward in dressing up and having the hair done. She was increasingly particular about her appearance, and about the house, and still more careful not to jump into action at a casual phone-call. For almost a year now she had been able to assure herself that she enjoyed the absolute freedom of her very lonely life.

He was in Dublin, he said, for his sister's funeral—his only return to Dublin in over thirty years. There was no one else, not even a cousin; he was the last of his clan. His sister had not married. A regular old maid, hadn't even a phone in the house. He was phoning from next door. He had had to get Lucy's phone number from Directory Enquiries since there was no single phone-book any more.

"I thought I recognised the voice," Lucy lied politely.

"Yours hasn't changed at all," he said, "but then, you didn't go away, did you?" There was a jeering inflection in his voice.

Well, no, Lucy thought, but I grew old. My voice must have changed. "Shouldn't I go to the funeral? I remember your sister."

"How would you get here?" he asked.

"I drive," Lucy answered equably. "The village is not on a bus-route like it used to be, but you are forgetting it is only thirty miles west of Dublin."

"You drive? You have a car? At your age?" There did not seem to be any humour in his voice. Lucy could not remember if tact and subtlety had been aspects of his character, but, of course, he was young then. She could only remember his face. A very handsome face with clear grey eyes.

"Have they changed all the roads out there?" he asked.

"Yes," Lucy answered, "the main road is a motorway now with junctions, and it is well signposted. But what about your sister's funeral, may she rest in peace. I would like..."

"No," he interrupted. "Forget it. Don't bother. Apart from a couple of old neighbours here, it will be a miserable affair. Stay where you are. I will come out to you the day after the funeral—the day after tomorrow." He had assumed that he was invited and would be made welcome. That was the moment when Lucy should have had the ready-to-hand excuse, not that he gave her the opportunity: "I'll see you, then," he said and rang off.

Lucy made a cup of coffee which she carried into a sunny window-alcove the better to sit and consider how could she now get out of an unwelcome visitor. His sister, the Lord have mercy on her, had moved to Dublin after their parents died. She had a job there, Lucy thought, but that was years ago. "Ringing from next door" left her no way of getting back on the phone to say she had remembered a previous engagement. Even if the dead sister had a phone, the number would be hard to find because there were probably dozens of Reillys in the book. Jim Reilly! Imagine!

By the time Lucy had finished the coffee, she had resigned herself. It was not, she told herself, that she would refuse hospitality to an old friend (or was he an old flame?), rather that she should refuse entry to an unknown force disturbing the serene course of her day.

The possibility that the triumphal bridge she had built from lonely adversity to proud independence had only the strength of a child's house of cards was a possibility firmly kept at bay.

He arrived in a taxi which, thought Lucy, must have cost quite a lot. Out here in the country, would he be able to get a taxi to take him away later in the evening? Lucy hoped so, but a small buzz-saw of anxiety started at the edge of her peace of mind.

"You are very welcome, Jim," which was no more than Lucy said to any guest. Only, in this case, it was not true. His appearance shocked her.

"I should hope so," and again she noticed a jeering edge on his voice. Rather than stare at his face, seeking a remembered feature, Lucy made gestures and phrases of hospitality, indicating the armchair by the fire and pushing the tray of whiskey and glasses to within his reach.

"Do help yourself, please. Or would you prefer gin?"

"No, this will do."

"A mixer? Ginger ale?"

"The jug of water here will do."

Somehow, the "will do" was ungracious. Lucy stole a look at his face while he poured out his whiskey. She would scarcely have known him. She had not seen, or imagined, so grim a visage. Apparently, he had never thought to groom his eyebrows. They grew down over his eyelids in a white wiry tangle. The clear grey eyes that Lucy remembered were now mere slits of no colour. His mouth, too, was different—the lips had fallen in. Didn't he have a rather sensuous mouth? A mouth that invited kisses and kissed most deliciously in return? Didn't he? There were some sensations of youth that you never forget. She couldn't be thinking of someone else, could she? There had not been a string of boy-friends in Lucy's girlhood. Thirty-five years ago it was a different world: much hardship, less freedom.

"You don't change much. You look well." He had a voice that would not invite coy contradiction. Lucy smiled a little. Then he added, "You've had it easy." He glanced around the comfortable room from under the barricades of his eyebrows.

"Yes," Lucy said. "Now tell me about yourself." Her instinct warned her to agree with everything this bitter-voiced, grim-faced man would say. The instinct was not exactly fear, not exactly disquietude, but rather a trace of self-preservation. Her life had not indeed been easy. Not easy at all. There had been a big family to rear, and a husband whose health had never been the best. There had been endless worry, but none of it for present discussion with Jim Reilly. "You have been in England all these years?"

"Yes," he said. "Scratching a living."

He refilled his glass. Lucy supposed he had forgotten that the Irish equivalent of politeness is to ask: "What are you having yourself?" He was content to drink alone.

"Are jobs very hard to get in England?" Lucy was easy with small-talk.

"They were, thirty years ago." He stared down into his whiskey. "I was a navvy, remember? In Woolwich."

In the deep dungeon of Lucy's memory something stirred. A prisoner, incarcerated for thirty years, stretched and sighed. Her hand went to her face as if to cover the shame of forgetting. "Yes," she said gently, "you went to England. You believed you would succeed in England. Everyone was going to England...in the years after the war."

His voice was as hard as his face. "At twenty-two years of age I was a get-rich-quick merchant. And it could have happened if you had kept your promise."

The prisoner in the dungeon must have expired on that last sigh. Lucy could remember nothing, nothing at all, beyond his going to England. Earlier skitting about, a little maybe. But a promise? What promise? Thousands went to England in those years.

"I see I have stirred up your recollection," he told her. "I have your letters still. I kept them. They are the only love-letters I ever got in my life." His voice had not softened. "Every day for nearly a year, you wrote. Then nothing. Nothing. Nothing. Why?"

Lucy hung her head and racked her brain. The vision of her wedding day came into full colour behind her eyelids. Her mother, her father, Donal's fine-drawn happy face. He was not long out of the sanatorium, and supposed to be cured of tuberculosis. Hadn't she written to Donal in the sanatorium? But love-letters every day for a year? And he had them to prove it? Or so he said.

"What happened?" Jim Reilly asked insistently. "What happened so suddenly?" Lucy had no idea. Did he answer all those letters? Lucy tried to picture her mother's face if, day after day, a letter from England dropped on the mat. What year was Donal in the sanatorium? Could it have been a question of which young man needed the more sympathy? Lucy had completely forgotten—hard to believe but a fact, whether this man accepted it or not. What was there to say?

"I had worked overtime around the clock to save the money to bring you over. To get to work cheaply, to save the extra, I had to go through the Woolwich Tunnel. In wintertime, in bitter cold, I hurried on the footpath of the Woolwich Tunnel, five o'clock in the morning and ten o'clock at night. Thousands of us pushing through the Woolwich Tunnel; in summertime sweating like pigs, fighting to get ahead to beat the clock. Five minutes late and you lost a half-hour. Through it again at night, frantic to get a few hours' sleep. Thirty years ago, the Woolwich Tunnel saved a couple of pounds a week and that was money then. It was a challenge, an adventure, while I had your letter warm with promise safe in the pocket of my donkey-jacket. Then you stopped. No reason given. Why?"

Had he come all this way in an expensive taxi, not for the pleasure of seeing her but to ask that question for which Lucy had no ready answer. Sometimes, when she was unable to sleep and lay awake half-dreaming, sometimes when she stood at the window on a sunny morning and gazed across the fields, memory would come unfolding back in an easy way, rolling film-like through her mind, picturing the children when they were little, small triumphs they had had. Happy memory, mostly. With Jim Reilly staring at her through those buried eyes, all memory went blank.

"I knew you were a widow," he said. "I was looking for a queue of wealthy suitors on the road." The jeer again?

Lucy thought of the urgent loneliness that had permitted her to accept invitations to dinner...from several widowers, in the first years after Donal's death. Elderly widowers they were, gone sadly downhill in the matter of personal hygiene, neglected men looking for a mother figure.

"You are taking your time with the answers," he

said and he topped up the whiskey, adding a drop of water. "So why did the letters stop? Don't invent. I have waited a long time for the truth. You knew I couldn't write much. What was there to write about? Starting in the Works at six, and hard at it until ten or eleven at night. The contractors were always to a deadline, all that stuff bombed-out in the war. I had no time for letters. But your's—they kept me alive—kept me going. Then you stopped. I waited. I waited. Jesus—I waited. Well?"

Did no one ever get a few days' holiday thirty-five years ago? If he had come over, Euston to Holyhead, would he have lost his job on the Woolwich Tunnel?

"Was there no other way you could have gone to work," she asked, "only through the Woolwich Tunnel?"

"The digs I got were on the south side of the Thames. The job I got was on the north side. The job paid. The digs were cheap. Yes, there was a steam ferry. You went on foot through the Woolwich Tunnel—it cost nothing. There were seven days in the week, you know. In those days a shilling counted."

To listen to his voice was hard on the ear. In Lucy's quiet fire-lit room, his voice was a heavy stone beating on an iron door. Thud. Thud.

"Was there no lodging you could get nearer to your work?"

Now his voice jeered her. "I had a lot of time to look for fancy lodgings in that year, hadn't I? The digs were dirt-cheap. She was a poor Czechoslovak woman married, or living with, a brute of a fellow who worked in the arsenal at Woolwich. She couldn't speak the lingo, even the rubbish he talked.

He beat the living daylights out of her every Saturday. And he beat the kid, a wretched little thing, about ten years old when I went there first."

Suddenly, Lucy remembered Jim Reilly's pious dead sister at mass with his respectable mother and father every Sunday in the parish church. Helen O'Dowd (dead this many years, poor Helen), who would do anything for a laugh, always pointed them out as "Lucy's future in-laws!" Other memories awoke. "Helen O'Dowd said the guards were looking for you?"

He gave what passed for a laugh. "You don't look senile," maybe his jeer was meant to be humour, and he seemed to be looking her over with wry-faced contempt. "But you cannot have forgotten that I laid out our mutual friend, Donal Creedon, in a fight in that pub at the end of the village. What was the name of it? Something Arms? They had to take Creedon away in an ambulance. My father had me on the mail-boat that night."

"Why did you hit him?" All the remembrances of Donal's ill-health rose up in his defence. Donal was never one for pub-brawling.

"Because, as I am damn sure you remember, he had the gall to object to my getting you in a clinch."

"I am going to put the kettle on," Lucy said. He did not follow her to the kitchen. She looked at the tray she had prepared: dainty sandwiches, her good fruit cake, the best china teacups. She felt she would like to crash it down on his head. That *would* be senile, and it would accomplish nothing. She must see this evening off to a safe conclusion. She must not disagree with or enrage a man of that type. Lucy, waiting for the kettle to boil, saw herself in a new light. It was not during the years since Donal's death that she had succeeded in carving out a path suitable to her nature and of settling tranquilly to each day. She had been attuned to that philosophy all her life. Dealing with Donal's recurring tuberculosis, feeding the family somehow when Donal went on half-pay, investigating all the possible ways to get the children fully educated by scholarships and grants. It is how I am, concluded Lucy in some surprise. My life has been a long apprenticeship. Accepting Jim Reilly's phone-call had revealed the vulnerability of a woman who still hoped. As she carried in the tea-tray, Lucy's sensibility was coping with the effort to regain her hard-won place on the precipice-ledge of loneliness.

Jim Reilly was hungry. He wolfed the food. When Lucy had taken away the tray she replaced the whiskey at his elbow. He pushed the whiskey further off. "That's enough for today," he muttered. He took out cigarettes, then put the packet away.

Lucy was intent on playing the kindly, slightly aloof, hostess. "Are you still in the same area in England? Do you still live in the same place?"

He eyed her. "Are you going to show me over the rest of your house?" he asked.

"Of course," Lucy said although his abruptness caused an apprehensive tremor of fear. "Go ahead," she said, "here is the staircase, and upstairs you will see three bedrooms, a room that was once a playroom, only my sewing-machine is there now, and the bathroom is upstairs also."

When he came down, he walked into the kitchen where she was putting away the dishes.

"All very comfortable, and well-kept." He did not

praise, he assessed. He looked out of the window. "Nice garden."

There was nothing to do but follow him into the sitting-room, fix the fire, and sit down politely. He watched her movements. She had dressed carefully, and set her wavy hair softly, but she had no feeling of being attractive. From this man she need never fear an approach, an offer of tenderness. The acid of his circumstances had eaten away any natural generosity of spirit he may have had.

"You were asking me," he said. "Yes, I remained in the same situation. For twelve years, I went through the Woolwich Tunnel twice a day. Twelve years is a long time to wait for a letter. A long time to face rejection. No letters to warm me. I substituted whiskey. I still took the ending of hope in and out of Woolwich, every day for twelve years."

He thought he had a monopoly on desperation. Lucy was tempted to tell him that her Donal endured his own Woolwich Tunnel—an endless vaulted nave of pain, years and years of retching blood, an eternity of sleepless, sweating nights. She said nothing.

"Then her old man beat her to death. There was no one to take care of the kid. The same kid since I went there. She was twenty-two when her bastard of a father was sentenced for life. She never had a chance. A bit soft in the head. A decent little body. Devoted to me."

"Was the girl able to go out to work? To get a job?"

"I got her a job on a cash-and-carry slot as a checker. After a while, I made her go on the bus, the ferry was finished. The Woolwich Tunnel was too much for her. We got a room with a kitchen and a toilet. She is a Catholic. I married her."

"So tell me about her? Her name?" Lucy's manner was now pleasantly at ease. Married. That was a relief.

The grimness of his face and his voice had not relaxed.

"Her name? Oh she has a long Czechoslovak name. I call her Bobo."

"And do you have a family?"

"Dead-born, all of them."

"Please accept my sympathy," Lucy put out a hand to touch his arm. He did not notice. He said, "They were not yours. I did not care."

Lucy was shocked into silence. Instinct warned her not to say "But they were yours." In silence, she grieved for poor Bobo and her dead-born babies.

"It was after that, I insisted she go on the bus, and not through the Woolwich Tunnel. And, probably as a result of those deaths, we were given a council house in one of the new towns."

"Is it nice?" Lucy asked, relieved to change the subject.

He looked around Lucy's sitting-room in which much of what was solidly comfortable had come from Lucy's grandparents along with the house and the bit of land. He looked out of the windows where the chestnut trees were changing colour. He looked at Lucy's bookcases, filled with Donal's books.

"It is not like this," he said, "and my wife is not like you."

There was an accusation in this statement, and Lucy resented it. "But Bobo is there. You have each other. You are not alone."

"She is there," he assented, and each harsh word

was thudding like a thrown rock. "She is there, in her wheelchair, and she has not spoken for years."

Lucy was unaware that he had ordered the cabman to return at seven-thirty. There were no words of thanks, nor of farewell. When the taxi came, he went. He had said what he came to say.

Sea Horses

A story for Dora Gibney

The only love-story Essy knew, when she was a little girl, was Sara's love-story. For a long, long time Essy accepted without question that it was a happy love-story which must end in happy-ever-after. Cinderella and Rapunzel and all the other stories in Essy's books all ended in brave rescues and love and kisses.

There were not any loving kisses in Essy's house in a Dublin back-street. She was given reasons to understand why. Her silent, tight-lipped mother had been left a widow with a child to bring up. Working all day in a Dublin factory, she was too busy, too poor, too hard-worked and too tired for Essy's endless questions. It took many, many years for Essy to understand that, indeed, her mother had loved her. All Essy wanted, when she was ten, were the words her mother never said.

With Sara, there was a world of love for Essy. When she was ten years old, she was got ready for her first holiday with Sara in Glentra, in Donegal. There were two new dresses, a new bathing-togs, new vests and new knickers, a new warm jersey, a new raincoat, a sou'wester hat. The same new things had to be bought every year for the holiday in Glentra. Her mother would sigh heavily, "Nothing from last year fits you. Only maybe the old hat?" and she would examine it closely: "It wouldn't keep out the rain any more," she would say regretfully.

"Maybe it won't rain this year?" Essy would offer hopefully.

"It always rains in Donegal," her mother said bitterly. And she would know, Essy thought; wasn't her mother born and reared in Glentra, the eldest of nine of whom Sara was the youngest?

"I don't care if it rains!" Essy sang out happily.

Her mother always looked at her critically. "You don't care about anything, Essy."

That wasn't true though Essy was always afraid to contradict.

Until Essy was fifteen, her mother brought her to the station in Dublin for the train to Donegal. Her mother carried the small suitcase up to the last minute. Then, before pushing Essy into the train she would whisper furtively, "Be sure to give Sara the packet the instant you arrive. Be sure now." Essy knew there was what her mother called "good money" in the packet carefully hidden under the clothes in the suitcase. Her mother did not say it was "holiday money": there was no letter, no exchange of fond nostalgia. To Essy's mother, good money in a packet was her expression of family solidarity for which she did not need language.

There were several changes on the journey. After Pettigoe, a smaller train brought them to Donegal town. Now the accents of the passengers had completely changed so Essy could almost believe she was in a foreign land. A kindly woman showed her where the omnibus stood waiting for passengers to Killybegs. There her Uncle Miko would be waiting for the "run down," as he called it, to Glentra.

Her uncle Miko was the one in her mother's family who had done well for himself. He owned an old Ford car. In Glentra village, he had the shop and the pub. The aroma of spirits and spice was always about him. Essy liked him. He always kept a ten-shilling note handy to slip into her pocket. That bought a birthday present for Sara's birthday which came mid-way through the two months' holiday.

The journey from Dublin took a whole day. After Killybegs and Kilcar, evening light filled the sky.

"What sea is that out there?" Essy asked Uncle Miko on the first unforgettable visit.

"That is Donegal Bay," he answered, "and only for the mist coming up, you would see Carrigan Point's high cliffs. And up there, blotting out the sky now, is Balbane. I climbed it often and I a gossoon."

"And what comes after Donegal Bay?" she wanted to know. Uncle Miko laughed at her ignorance. "Sure that is the Atlantic going on over to America, or Newfoundland, where I have a brother, your Uncle Francie. I named my eldest for him."

Essy was filled with awe at the immense wonder of it all. It seemed an infinity of space. And to have an uncle in a new found land? Her mother never told her that.

If the journey was long, the end was worth waiting for.

When the car drew up at the cottage in Glentra, Sara was there with her arms spread wide to take Essy and give her all the loving kisses and hugs and giggles that her childish heart so longed for from one year to the next. That longing never changed. To be pressed warmly against Sara's soft bosom was the prize at the gates of Heaven. Somewhere in the shadowy doorway behind Sara, her husband Tomás was standing like Saint Peter.

In that first year when Essy was ten, Sara was twenty-two. She had been married to Tomás for five years.

"No baba at all yet!" she told Essy happily as she stowed away the precious packet of money and then placed the new clothes on two shelves in the loft room. "You can be my childeen now for two whole months. We'll be *ag stealladóireacht* in the sea every day. I see you have the outfit for it with you," she was holding up the new bathing-togs. "I haven't one of them *stiall uisce* at all. But sure I can wear an old gansy of Tomás. Who'll see us? And we in the bay below the house. The *madradh*, Ruk, will bark for warning! Isn't it the fine sight a stray visitor would have and two *cailíní* in the water!"

"Doesn't Uncle Tomás go in?" Essy asked.

"He never learned to swim," she said, "and him out fishing in the sea near every day."

Her mother had said it always rains in Donegal. Essy remembered a mist moving in off the sea, and turning the quartzite mountain slope of Befan into a curtain of mauve. She remembered dawn-clouds so grey they were like enormous pearls on a silver rope. She remembered cliffs of heather turning from red to pink, and brilliant fuchsias hanging with great drops of moisture. But she remembered much more the vivid sunshine on the golden strand below the cottage. She remembered Sara throwing off the gansy and lying flat out on the rocks to dry in the sun. She felt no shame in staring at Sara's perfect body and Sara felt no shyness in Essy's staring. Essy longed to touch but she never dared. Intimacy was a wonderment. The infringement of intimacy would lose the prize at the gates of Heaven. Essy took off the bathing-togs and Sara did not seem ever to notice.

What did they talk about in those first few summers? Essy never remembered if they bothered to talk at all. They frolicked around the little bay. They helped Tomás with the turf. One year, on a calm, cloudless beautiful day, they went with Tomás in his currach for a picnic to the island of Rathlin O'Birne. Another year, Uncle Miko took Sara and Essy to see the high cliffs of Slieve League. To hear him talk boastfully of how they were the highest maritime cliffs in Europe, they might as well have been on his own land.

In the summer that Essy was thirteen, a summer of golden days in their little bay, she came out of the sea with blood on her legs. No one warned her and she was frightened. She was glad to be Sara's childeen that day and that night. Tomás was away at the fishing, and Sara gave her Tomás's place in the big bed.

The tenderness of Sara's body was indescribable. "*Ná bíodh buaidhreamh ort, mo sheoid,*" she whispered. "There need not be fear, jewel. It is what every woman gets, *gach mí*—yes, every month. *Mo mhamaí* says it readies up the *ubhagán* for the *páiste.*"

"I don't want a *páiste,*" Essy cried, "I'd rather be your *páiste,* your childeen like you said. What is an *ubhagán?*"

But Sara was not sure of the word in English, or in Irish. "We call it *ubhagán,*" she said, "it is a *neidín,* a little nest in a woman, where the *páiste* is safe until it comes *amach* into the world."

Essy had heard of birds' nests in trees, but she had never seen one. Sara's body, close to her drew a long, sad sigh. Essy turned sideways to her.

"Are you crying, Sara? What's wrong?"

"*Níl mé ag gol*," she sighed again, "only thinking do I have the *ubhagán* myself."

"Don't you bleed every month?"

"*Am agus am eile*," she said in a puzzled voice, "not every month."

Sara did not offer a solution to the mysterious tanglements of bleeding and bringing a baby to birth. Instead, snuggling into the warmth of the bed, she told her own story.

Sara fell in love when she was fifteen. Colum was seventeen. Sara's parents, Essy's grandparents, were not rich, but his parents were dirt-poor. Sara's parents had a house for their nine children. They had a good roof over their heads. As they were reared, they were got off to America. They sent money home. The boy's parents were feckless. Their children only half-raised, the parents were sent to the workhouse. The family split and scattered. Sara's boy stayed. He worked on the bog, on the roads, on the sea. He was trying to put the few shillings together to go to Scotland where he would get farm-work, or even snagging or picking in the season. He had the fare got for himself, only not enough for Sara to go with him.

"After all were in bed and unconscious with sleep," Sara whispered for fear the walls might hear this secret, "I crept out to be with him. He was gaunt with the hunger. I wrapped my cloak around him and we lay down in the furze. 'If I got you with child,' he said to me and his hands warming themselves inside my shift, 'the priest would have us to be married and we could go away respectable, and you wouldn't be crying for the harm done to your family.'

" 'It is not a child coming would change my father,' I told him, 'it is because of your father being put in the poorhouse. My father has his pride.' He said, 'Couldn't you let me anyway?' And he was begging me, and I was wanting to have him in the *neidín* where the child would be coming, and I was wanting and wanting and wanting. I could only cry and cry, 'I can't, Colum, I can't.' I was full of pity for him. He was starving to put up the few shillings for Scotland. He begged and begged but he did not force me."

The boy did not force her. Her parents did. Her mother had told her that her father had a pride that could split stones. Before Lent of that year, a match was made for Sara with a sensible man, Tomás Gallagher.

"It was a long, long ceremony," Sara told Essy. "Beginning with the nuptial mass, and then the long prayers for us two to prosper, and prayers for our parents who had kept us in the faith, and then prayers for the dead belonging to us, and more prayers for the dead souls in purgatory (and all the time, the terrible noise went on, deafening our ears) and then the priest (who was an uncle of Tomás on the mother's side) he gave a long sermon. And all the time, we were standing up to the altar in our new clothes, all the time we could hear the hooves. A horse was being ridden and ridden and ridden on the stones outside around the chapel. Around and around and around. And when we went forward to take the marriage vows, through the side window and level with the proud face of my father, I could see the horse and the rider every time he went galloping past. It was Colum, childeen, Colum. And he rode and rode and rode that old spavined horse that used to draw their turf. The horse and the rider streaming sweat. Pounding on and on around the chapel until the long ceremony was over. Thundering out beyond where I saw my father's face set like the tombstones in the *roilig*." The sobs rose in Sara's throat to be quelled with her final words: "And I saw the tombstones where my grandmother and her mother and women belonging to me for generations, were all buried—all sold to men for a lease of their lives. Sold as I was being sold—for a bullock and a few fields of turf."

This was a different Sara from the Sara who splashed below in the bay. Essy crept closer to her, recognising the same bitterness she saw in her mother. The bitter blood of poverty was in their veins, and it was more than that, more than she could know then. She wanted Sara to be joyously uncaring, running into the tide, and lazing her body on the flat rocks.

"What happened to Colum?" she whispered.

"No one knows, acushla. He was never seen in the townland again."

The year Essy passed seventeen, she left school.

"This will be your last holiday in Donegal," her mother said. "You must get a job when you come back."

"Yes, yes, I will," Essy answered quickly, "Oh I

will. I will." She did not want her mother to spoil the day by the sad story of the years of slavery and sacrifice. Essy knew, but the sacrifice seemed to diminish by the repetition of the telling.

This year, Sara would have her thirtieth birthday. Essy had made great secret plans for the day, saving as much as she could from the odd jobs after school—mostly minding other people's children. She felt she could have left school at fifteen to earn this kind of money had not her mother set such a value on finishing the education properly. Her mother could go on forever about the value of education.

Nothing had changed in Glentra. It was always *Tír na nÓg*, the land of youth. Sara was as slim and tanned as ever, her thick hair as black, her eyes as green. Tomás looked even more like Saint Peter because his hair was grizzled with grey. He was a silent man, but never unkind.

The prize at the gates of Heaven was still there for Essy. Sara held her closely and tenderly, kissing her face and laughing softly to see Essy close her eyes with love.

It was another of those wonderful summers. Day after day, they sunned themselves on the wide flat rocks. To a girl not yet eighteen, thirty seems like middle age, but Essy could see no change in Sara's body. She was still perfect and Essy still longed to caress her. She loved Sara too much to be jealous about her but sometimes Essy needed reassurance.

"Do you love Tomás any more than you did, Sara?"

"How could I, childeen, when I never loved him at all?" and Sara's voice was careless.

"But you sleep together?" Essy prompted.

"Oh aye!" Sara said, a little wearily.

"Do you like it when he makes love to you?"

Sara laughed, her head thrown back, her black hair streaming in the breeze from the sea. "Make love!" she repeated, "make love! You are full of new words. Dublin words, *an eadh?*"

"They are the words in books," Essy said defensively.

"*Óinsín!*" Sara laughed, "there is no such thing *as déanamh grádh*. In Donegal there is *déanamh airgid*. People can make money, they cannot make love."

Sara leaned from her rock to push Essy gently.

It was a gesture of affection. "I wish you were ten again! You were much nicer—not so curious—and we could have the years all over again."

They were quiet for a little time.

"But what are you asking?" said Sara. "What harm. I'll answer: *seo an freagra. Ta slí agam*—what is that word? Aye, a method. I never turn my back to Tomás, *an dtuigeann tú?* I never refuse him. A woman cannot do that. It is *peacach*. Yes, it is in the catechism. *Mo mháthair agus mo shean-mháthair agus an sagart* all said it. It is in the catechism. *An slí* then. I lie in bed the way I lie on this rock and I listen to the horse like the waves below – thundering around and around the chapel. And I wonder then if I had run out of that chapel and jumped up on the horse behind Colum, where would I be today? That is the dream keeps me occupied the while Tomás, *bíonn sé ag cuireadh isteach é – gan iarraidh fós*." Without skill, without words, Tomás possessed Sara.

Essy grew up in that moment. All the possibilities and the probabilities of the world went surging through her mind, stinging as nettles sting. Sinful to refuse a husband? Grievously sinful? Mortally sinful? But to ignore a husband while he...while he...? At seventeen Essy knew there had to be a making of love.

"Is that fair, Sara?" Essy gasped, almost in dismay.

"It is all I know!" Sara retorted. "*Is cuma liom!*"

But Essy knew she did care. *Is cuma liom* was easy to say if you could not admit to the bitterness running deeply within. Essy recognised again her mother, Hester, in Sara. They were alike in that both women had been deprived of love and of life.

Then Sara began to laugh, careless as ever. She pulled Essy to her feet, she held her closely for just a second, and then they were running into the water.

"*Tar liom! Tar liom!*" Sara called out merrily. "*Tar liom 'un na fairrge!* The tide will wash away our thoughts."

Sara's birthday was a day of brilliant sunshine. Essy had arranged with Uncle Miko to bring them to Killybegs in his new "motoring-car." as Sara called it. Tomás came that far with them. He was going with the other fishermen up beyond Tory Island. They watched as the big fishing-boats sailed with the rising tide.

"They will likely be gone a week," Sara told Essy.

From Killybegs, there was the old bus into Donegal town. Here they would spend the day going around the shops and the ancient monastery where the Four Masters wrote their histories.

"Like two returned Yanks the pair of you," said Uncle Miko, slipping a couple of notes into Essy's pocket. He would collect them back from Killybegs in the evening.

Sara looked splendid as they walked around the little town inspecting the shops for Sara's present. Essy saw men turn to look at Sara. She was bare-legged, her feet in sandals, a green *cábóg* perched on her lustrous black hair. Her spun skirt was as green as her eyes and her hat. When they were eating the special birthday dinner in the Abbey Hotel, Essy noted (and never forgot) the pink bloom of Sara's cheeks.

From Killybegs to Kilcar, the road runs close enough to the coast for the expanse of Donegal Bay to draw the eyes away out to the Atlantic, there to gaze in wonder at the great panorama of sunset in the western sky. On Sara's birthday, the return journey to Glentra revealed no lovely sunset at the end of so lovely a day.

"By gor," said Uncle Miko, "there's a dirty-looking load of squall up there! We'll have rain surely."

When Uncle Miko put them down at the head of the boreen, the first jagged streak of lightning split the sky.

"Run, let ye!" he roared from the car as he reversed hurriedly.

They made no move to go to bed. The noise of the storm would have made sleep impossible. Sara used the bellows on the fire, piling on the turf, and they sat in the hollowed-out *súgán* chairs, drugged with the heat.

The lightning lit up the kitchen every few minutes, followed by thunder claps so terrifying they seemed to break directly above the cottage.

"Would the cottage blow into the sea?" Essy asked Sara.

"'Twill never stir," she said. "Tomás has the roof bound and weighted. His father and him do it every other year, with fresh thatch added, and Befan rises up behind it for a shelter."

The dog, Ruk, was an outside dog but tonight Sara had let him share the fireside. She played with his ears and he turned adoring eyes on her.

"I would like if Ruk is in every night," Sara said, "But Tomás says he is out for a guard. Tomás says it was his grandfather gave him *an madradh* and named him Ruk. It was Tomás's great-great-grandfather built this house."

"Would that be a hundred years?" Essy wondered.

"Oh aye," Sara smiled, "and more than a hundred, I'm thinking."

She had never before mentioned Tomás three times in the one breath.

The storm blew itself out by morning. They never went to bed at all, and they heard it moving away. At six o'clock, the sun was coming up brilliantly like the morning before. Sara wet the tea and they stood at the door, mugs in their hands, watching the little surf-topped waves rushing in, sucking back, and rushing in again. Sara was very quiet.

"Are you tired, Sara?" Essy asked.

Sara's smile was wan, and when she answered, her voice was barely above a whisper. "Inside in my head is all *tré na chéile*, childeen. Would you think of stepping up to Miko's shop, and ask him is there *scéala*. News, is that the word? News, is it?"

Then Essy remembered Tomás. Sara must be thinking of the fishermen out in the fierce storm.

"Will you come too?" Essy asked.

"I'll stop here," she said. She put the mug down on the step.

Essy looked back to wave from the top of the slope. Sara was huddled into her shawl, her head turned resolutely towards the sea.

Long afterwards, Essy thought that Sara knew in that first hour.

At Uncle Miko's shop, there was a gathering of women and children. They were not keening yet, that would come later; now there was no hope in their faces. Experience had taught them that when boats go missing off the Donegal coast lives will be lost. There will be widows and orphans.

Essy's grandmother's face was peaked with anxiety. She questioned Essy: "Sara stopped behind to watch the sea? It is *mí-ádh* to take the eyes off the water. Her thoughts on him, her thoughts must go with him. Is that for luck, *stóirín*? Is that the word for it?" She began to moan "Athach gaoithe! Athach!".

"We heard it all night, *a Mháthair Mhór*. What will I tell Sara?"

There were seven, maybe eight, boats missing. A score of men would drown, the women moaned, the townland of Glentra be bereft.

Uncle Miko put up a bag of groceries and a bottle of poteen. His son carried the bag as far as the boreen.

"The old people always say that whatever way the currents run around Tory, the men are seldom found," he told Essy.

"Do you mean, Francie, that their bodies do not get washed ashore?"

"They get washed away to the North where there is always snow. The old people say that the currents of the wind and the currents of the ocean conspire against them. If a man is found, it is a rare thing if they can tell if it is the same man."

"Would he be a skeleton?" Essy asked fearfully.

"There's rarely bodies for a funeral," Francie said as he handed over the bag. He was not willing to go further with bad news. For Sara, he muttered, it was a *droch-scéal, ana-droch-scéal*.

After three weeks of waiting, morning, noon, and night; and lighting candles in the chapel; and praying endless rosaries and the priest reciting the Salve Regina after the daily mass, there was still no news of the missing fishermen. If their boats broke up in the storm, the old people said it might be a year before a recognisable spar could come in on the tide. The keening of the women *gan scéal, gan scéal fós*, went on in every *bothán*.

"There are some here," Essy's grandmother said, "who will not give up hope to the end of their days, *go ndéanfaidh Dia trócaire ortha*."

At last the priest ordained that there would be a solemn requiem mass for the missing men. Everyone left in the parish would attend.

The chapel was packed with people. They were walking up the aisle, looking for a place, when Essy saw Sara give a start and a kind of a shudder. She gripped Essy's hand and urged her forward. When they were kneeling, Essy's hand was still gripped. Sara used her other hand to draw her shawl closer around her face.

" 'Tis him," she breathed in amazed awe, " 'tis him. He is here. 'Tis Colum."

The man who was Colum was standing at the chapel gate when they came out. Sara had insisted on delaying to say fifteen decades of the rosary long after the mass was finished. The man had waited. He was standing there, tall and arrogant.

Why shouldn't the man Colum stand there in his well-cut clothes? Even if he had not been seen in Glentra for thirteen years? Hadn't he come to offer his sympathy to one he had loved? Why shouldn't he step forward and place his hand on the arm of the shawled woman whose face was wet with tears?

Essy had never lost sight of the happy-ever-after for her beloved Sara.

Why did Sara recoil, and push Essy forward so they must hurry away?

Sara's first instinct, after the storm, had told her that she was already a widow. Her first instinct, when she saw Colum, was an instinct of fear.

"I have my car," Colum said, "I will drive you up to the bay."

Sara pushed Essy in front of her, their bare feet skimming the stones.

Late that night, when Essy was in bed up in the loft room, and Sara was screening the turf embers for morning, there was the sound of a car pulling over the *screag*. The cottage door was never locked, and now it was pushed open. Essy heard Sara's swift intake of breath, and it seemed that Colum had taken Sara into his arms for there was a soft sound of a struggle. Then, in a moment, the creaking noise of the old settle by the window-wall. Colum had laid Sara on the settle and she was not struggling any more.

They spoke totally in the tongue of their childhood. Only when he raised his voice could Essy hear the words repeated: "*Is liom-sa thú. Is liom-sa thú.*" Yes, Sara belonged to him. She had never ceased to belong to him. She had acquiesced, merely acquiesced, to Tomás.

Essy fell asleep at last, lulled by the heavy pounding of the incoming tide...the horses' hooves of drowned Tomás's love-making.

In the months that followed, Essy wrote to Sara many times. There was no answer. She wrote to her grandmother in Glentra, then to her Uncle Miko, and to her cousin Francie. There was never an answer.

"You would think they were all dead!" she complained to her mother.

"Dead you would hear about!" her mother said, shortly. "Disgrace is likely what it is. Your Aunt Sara is in disgrace would be my bet."

"It can hardly be a disgrace if she is a widow and marries Colum!" Essy did not often answer back to her mother.

"It would be if she didn't, though!" her mother said, abruptly closing the subject.

Essy was never to know how much, or how little, her mother ever knew about anything. Her mother considered a still tongue in the head to be a mark of "cleverality."

At Christmas, a card of holly and robins and a five-pound note went to Glentra in the customary way. The silence was not broken.

Christmas had almost come around again, when Essy's mother had a brief letter from Sara. She read it several times. Her face seemed suddenly older and more anxious. She handed the letter to Essy. The envelope had an English postmark, and on the letter there was no address and no date:

Dear Hester,

I am going on the mail boat. Can you meet the train in Westland Row? If it is not Thursday, it will be Friday. Love to Essy.

Your sister,

Sara.

"What will you do?" Essy asked, dreading that she would tear the miserable little letter into bits and throw it on the fire.

"I will meet the train, what else?" her mother replied sharply, "the two days if I have to. She is my sister."

Essy's mind teemed with tragic possibilities but her mother did not invite discussion. They turned out Essy's bedroom, and made it ready for Sara. There was a sofa-bed in the parlour for Essy while Sara would be with them.

Essy's mother took time off work to meet the mail-boat train that came in at five-thirty. Essy's job was to hurry home from her office to have the fire going and the kettle on the hob. They were to come on the tram from the station. In the event, Essy's mother took a cab because Sara was on the verge of collapse.

Essy's first sight of Sara was heart-wrenching. The beautiful Sara, the winsome Sara of *Tír na nÓg*, had become a creature of skin and bone.

Essy's mother put Sara to bed as she would put a beloved child. There was no luggage. A flannel nightdress that fitted Essy years before was found and warmed for Sara. She fell asleep almost immediately.

In the kitchen Essy's mother shut the door softly.

"Go to the doctor's surgery, Essy," she said, "tell him it is urgent tomorrow that he comes. Very urgent. Here is his fee for fear he might forget. I have the two days off. I will have her ready. You take my bed tonight. I'll sit with her."

The doctor's diagnosis was simple. Sara was dying of pulmonary tuberculosis. To Hester's entreaties he could only repeat that the hospitals were full of her sort already. He agreed to put her name on a waiting-list for a sanatorium.

"All you can do for your sister is keep her fresh: the sweats are severe at this stage. Plenty of fresh air, the window wide open."

"And nourishing food?" Hester asked in a pleading voice she had never used before.

"A little of what she might fancy," and the doctor went away, shaking his head sadly.

That night, Essy's mother came into the parlour where Essy was fixing the sofa-bed for the night. The girl was choked with rebellious tears. "I don't believe that doctor," she turned on her mother, "if we could get her back up to Glentra—up to the little bay, I..." The tears would not stay choked up.

Her mother ignored this outburst. "I should send you away from here," she said, "you will be next."

"I won't go!" Essy said vehemently, "I am staying wherever Sara is. I won't go anywhere."

Her mother was very quiet. At last, she said, "God help me. I am failing in my duty not to send you away. Whole families go down with the consumption contagion."

"I would rather die!" Essy burst out at her.

Her mother thought about that for a moment, then she said, in the same quiet voice, "Maybe we all would."

So it was arranged. Essy's mother went on night-work in the factory, where she had worked herself up to the position of forewoman. When Essy came in at five o'clock in the evening, her mother got a few hours' sleep. Essy brought her evening meal into Sara's room, and there she stayed until it was time to go to bed. Then there was a little bell to hand, on Sara's bed, just in case she needed anything.

In the first couple of weeks, Sara tried to talk. Essy wanted so much to know what had gone wrong with the happy-ever-after ending of Sara's love-story.

"But didn't you love Colum all the time?" Essy asked. "And, Sara, didn't he want you so much?"

"He wanted only his revenge, *stóirín*." And Sara's eyes filled with weak tears. Her eyes were like green tarns in her small, flushed face.

Soon, there was no more talk at all. Sara was content to watch Essy through lowered eyelids, her hand in Essy's hand, her clasp frailer each day. A murmured "childeen" was all she could say.

When Sara died, Hester drew out all the Post Office savings.

"We will take her home to Glentra, whether they welcome her or not. I have written the priest to have a place in the *roilig*, I sent the money. 'Tis where I would wish to go myself in God's good time. There will be a mass for the dead, as is proper. She has had the priest here to shrive her soul."

At Killybegs, Uncle Miko was waiting. He had his wife and Francie in the car. He followed the hearse, as did Hester's hired car. There was no sign of the grandparents. Hester spoke then.

"We will soon be at Glentra; and now I will tell you the things you should know. Colum had a wife left behind in Raphoe when he took Sara to England, a wife and a child of a few months. When she knew that fact in England, for the woman's father came after him, Sara stayed with him. That is the sin your grandfather will never forgive. And there is more than that he will not forgive. Colum tried to make Sara will him Tomás Gallagher's cottage on the bay, and the six acres of bog foreby—the acres that were belonging to your grandfather and given to Sara for her dowry. She would not make that new will for him. He tried to make her by beating her. And that was when she ran away. And now, Essy, I will tell you something that you will never tell a living soul. This must never pass your lips. Promise me solemnly, don't just nod your head: The Salvation Army took her in and 'twas they gave her the ticket to Dublin."

Essy could see now the grey stretches of Donegal Bay, westering away to America across the Atlantic. The sky was wintry. At that moment, it was not the scenic wonderland never far from Essy's imagination. It was more, far more, it was a home-coming to the place where Essy's heart would always be at home.

"You are not listening to me," her mother said.

"What did you say?" asked Essy, her eyes feasting themselves on the waters and the cliffs.

"I said: when Tomás Gallagher married your Aunt Sara, your grandfather got Tomás to make a will that the six acres would come back to Sara's family if Tomás died before Sara. There was always the danger of the sea."

"Grandfather will get them back, so," Essy said.

"He will not," her mother answered sharply, "because Sara got Tomás to put it in the will, long

55

long ago, that when Sara would die, the acres and the cottage would go to you."

Essy stared around at her mother in blank amazement.

"And that will cause bad feeling, too," Hester added with a kind of sour satisfaction.

Essy's mother did not live into old age, just long enough to see Essy happily married. When she died, Essy and her husband, Niall, brought her back to Glentra. Hester and Sara sleep together in the *roilig*, their names on the one grey stone...two sisters, the eldest and the youngest of a family now scattered across the world.

Summer after summer, Sara's cottage has been a refuge, and a holiday home for a whole generation: for Essy and Niall, for all their children, and now for their grandchildren. Soon, Niall will retire and they will live there.

Essy often stands at the door looking down to the bay, knowing the sea in all its changes. The last little grandchild, whose name is Sara, is playing happily on the sand. She has tied a trailing wrack of seaweed to her tiny blue shorts to make a horse-tail. She is galloping around and around, swishing the tail.

Forever in Hong Kong

Belle was not well-off. Her civil service pension barely covered the decent necessities. When it came to Christmas or birthdays with so many nieces and nephews, or, as now, when it came to finding the money for a good wedding present for her favourite niece, Belle was sadly at a loss to find the necessary money.

Today she had remembered a piece of furniture that was still in the bedroom she had as a girl. If it had no woodworm, perhaps she could have it polished and present it to Etta. She was very fond of Etta. They said Etta had the looks of Belle when Belle was young. It was nice that Etta was going to be married to her handsome young man.

Belle drew a cardigan around her shoulders for the climb up the second flight of stairs to her old bedroom. The house was cold in wintertime.

The piece of furniture did not look too bad, merely dusty. Nowadays these pieces were called tall-boys, but when Belle kept her things in it, it was called a chest-of-drawers. Belle examined it carefully. There was no woodworm. It was old-fashioned perhaps but it was made of solid mahogany. Commodious too with six drawers in deepening sizes. It was nicely finished with rope edges and shapely brass handles.

She tested the top drawer, drawing it smoothly towards her. It was empty except for a small cardboard box.

Belle held the little box in gentle fingers. It was shabby from long years of being laid away. The once-bright gilt lettering had almost faded:

THE NEW HENRY STREET ARCADE
WATCHES CLOCKS JEWELLERY

Inside this box, she thought (perhaps she murmured the thought because now she quite often thought aloud when she was alone, and that was almost always), here in this little box, all tucked away, are four years of my youth. Yes, four, from my eighteenth birthday until I was twenty-two. She nodded her head, a little sadly, in agreement with herself. Those were the years of Belle and Brian…Brian and Belle.

Belle's eighteenth birthday fell on August Monday Bank Holiday. She and Brian cycled to Rathfarnham. Then they had to join with dozens of other fellows and girls all pushing their bicycles the rest of the way up the steep hill to the Pine Forest.

"Everybody in Dublin seems to have the same idea as we have," Brian grumbled, "maybe we should have thought of somewhere else. Out to the sea at Portmarnock, perhaps?"

"But you said we would like the mountains best, didn't you?" Belle would have been happy any place with Brian. He was far and away bigger and better than anyone else she had ever seen. They had met only a month before her birthday, on the day they had both entered the civil service. Belle was sure their meeting was not a mere coincidence, it was fate. It was destiny that had arranged their meeting.

Belle felt certain that Brian recognised this great fact of destiny. Of course she did not expect him to say so because Belle understood men. She had three brothers and any sentence more fraught with meaning than "Pass the jam" was soppy to them. She had three sisters also, but they were still too young to understand the meaning of destiny.

"Give me your bicycle," Brian called over to her, "I can push the two together." Would a brother ever offer that?

Since Belle had met Brian, she had floated loose in a world of effervescent dreams of the future. But secret dreams. Her mother was apt to become meanly suspicious of what she called "idle wool-gathering." Belle had to hide her notions and bide her time.

To have this whole glorious day with Brian was an unhoped-for bonus before the long winter months when Brian planned to study for a higher grade in the civil service. Every night from Monday to Friday, he said, all winter long.

For this wonderful day, free from her family, Belle intended to let her dreams soar over the Dublin mountains. And perhaps, Belle thought, Brian would too.

Belle passed her fingers over and around the little box. Four years were trapped in that little box.

Belle's mother and father had disapproved of Brian from the start. Belle was far too young to have a boy-friend. Far too young to go steady. She thought, regretfully now, of all the battles she had fought against their disapproval during those four years. Battles to join *An Óige* and go weekend hostelling with Brian, they were big battles. Lesser battles to go to the civil service shindigs on a Saturday night, and lesser, but still battles, to go walking or to the cinema.

"Moonlighting" her father called it. Everything she wanted to do with Brian was "moonlighting." "It is a matter of principle, Belle," her father repeated constantly, "a matter of principle. If that young fellow had any respect for you..."

Everything in those days was a matter of principle. Belle's mother had similar fears about lack of respect. They never knew, they never even suspected, that on her eighteenth birthday, deep in the Pine Forest, Belle's virginity had vanished into the bed of heather beneath the pine trees.

"Will we always be together, always and always for ever?" an ecstatic Belle asked Brian as he lay there smiling at her.

"Of course, of course, you know we will."

"Even though we only know each other a month," persisted Belle, "Even though..."

Brian stopped further questioning with further kissing. In the time to come afterwards, Brian always stopped further planning with further love-making. Brian was a born love-maker, was Belle's admiring thought: he could never get enough of it.

Brian was ambitious too. He took classes and examinations in an ever-climbing progression towards his goal. Belle could not understand why her mother did not appreciate all the efforts Brian was making to rise up in the world.

"You are making a sorry mistake arranging your life around that fellow. You sit in all day and then go out at this hour of the night to meet him after his night-classes. Why can't he see himself home?"

Belle tried to be reasonable. She hated rows. She hated the acrimonious voices endlessly raised against her.

"It is the only time I see him, Mammy."

And hold him and love him and give in to his need of me.

Her father had to have his say, "Are you telling the truth that he is at his studies until this late hour?"

"Honest, Dad."

"Or do you wait outside a pub for him?"

But Brian did not drink, nor smoke. He was cautious with money.

Belle held the little box to her lips. She hoped the parents of today were not narrow-minded and mean. She had wanted to confide in her mother. She had to deceive her for Brian's sake, increasingly.

If they had trusted her, it would surely have been different. Towards the end of their lives they had stopped upbraiding her. They thought they had won. They had gained back a daughter who never afterwards left them. Their justification was undeniably to be found in the compensating comfort of an eldest daughter maturing into a spinster.

Belle weighed the little box, balancing it in the palm of her hand. Brian had risen steadily in the civil service. He never talked about his success nor did he have words for passionate love nor for his future life with Belle. She took it for granted that he was self-effacing, not forward and flirtatious like a lot of the fellows in the office. Several of the girls, who had come into the office more recently than she, married and had children. When she was twenty-one, it was assumed by the girls that Belle would be displaying an engagement ring, or at least a gold watch. There were covert jokes about old maids.

When Brian was twenty-one, his father had suggested that he get out and find a lodgings for himself. Belle had found one for him, a basement flat on Rathmines Road. She had painted it, and carpeted it, and curtained it. Secretly she had a vision that this cosy place might be their first home—their start in life.

Belle opened the little cardboard box. This was the watch which Brian had given her on her twenty-second birthday. It was not gold. It was not silver. Wistfully, she supposed it was tawdry and cheap even then.

"A present for you!" Brian said, "and read what it says on the box! Guaranteed for ever!"

Brian put it on her wrist as they lay in bed in the basement flat. She was conscious of the warmth of his body as she held up her arm to admire the watch. She snuggled against him to thank him, but the suitable words of gratitude did not come. A sense of childish disappointment threatened to assail her eyes with tears. The watch was a let-down. Any watch would have been a disappointment. She longed for a diamond ring—a great big ring that marked the full circle of approval for her years of bondage.

Holding back the tears made Belle go silent.

"Don't you like it?" Brian asked, but he did not wait for her reply. He was not as deeply concerned for her answer as for his own pleasurable satiation.

There had been so many hundred of nights of Brian and Belle that she could never afterwards be certain if that really was the last night of all?

They met again in broad daylight in Merrion Street. Brian was wearing a new suit. His hair was very groomed.

"Have you heard? I got the job!" He was all smiles, his eyes, his teeth, even the toes of his shoes were glistening.

What job, her eyes asked. He had not told her of another upward move.

"You must know," he said impatiently. "It is the one in the Department of External Affairs! They are posting me to Canberra!"

Strangely, bewilderingly, he was off down the street without a backward glance. Her life was over. When she was twenty-two, her life was over.

Belle returned the watch to its cardboard box. All those years ago, it had stopped after three weeks of wear.

She had taken it back to The New Henry Street Arcade.

"I did not drop it," she said earnestly, "It just stopped. And you can see, it is guaranteed for ever?"

The man behind the counter smiled, "I see that, and I also see it is made in Hong Kong. Now, isn't that nice? Made in Hong Kong and guaranteed for ever! I am sorry, Miss, but my years are not Hong Kong years."

But mine were, Belle murmured as she laid the little box back in the dusty drawer. Mine were, Brian. For ever and ever.

A Bona Fide Husband

He was driving carefully, in a carefully rehearsed, civil frame of mind, through a part of the city unfamiliar to him.

He had decided to visit her. He did not know how he had made the complete mental circle from total rejection to itching desire. He had persuaded himself that, at the least, the visit would give pleasure. She must be lonely.

He had taken a deal of trouble with his appearance. This had involved having his hair trimmed—a little office she had always done for him. He would be sure to tell her, in a jovial way of course, what money she had saved him down through the years; the barber-shop nowadays must make a fortune.

He had given a moment's thought to the bringing of a gift. Flowers, perhaps? She was a great one for bringing a gift when visiting. Casual gifts were not something he had approved of. Somewhat pretentious, he always said. Ah well, she surely had to forego such extravagances now—her means must be meagre enough. For which she had herself to thank. He let go the idea of a gift. Flowers were a thought too exotic for a plain man.

He had turned down off the South Circular Road.

Irritably, he now realised that he had come back twice into a street identical with all the other parallel back-to-back streets. It was enough to fray a man's temper. He was aware that his temper frayed easily—she had told him so often enough. He knew it was not so much his temper as her provocation. She could provoke him in a calm voice and then pretend childish wonder that he was shouting with loss of temper. Provocation was a fault she had never learned to curb. Living now in a maze of back-streets was typically provoking of her.

He pulled in the car to the pavement. He could keep his temper just as well as the next fellow. This was the time to appear cool, self-contained, self-sufficient, which essentially he was. He looked at the slip of paper on which he had written her address. That was the house all right. It stood in a long terrace of houses, street-level with a railed basement area. In the twilight, no one house seemed any less dreary than the other. He rapped sharply on the ancient knocker.

An amber light showed through the fanlight. Her voice asked, "Who is it?"

He almost retorted, "Jack the Ripper!" because her voice had flooded through him, casting out his taut humour and restoring him to what he recognised as his normal light geniality. In the same instant, he remembered she hated teasing. Summoning up a very sober voice, he replied, "John Blane."

The door-bolts were slid back, and the door was opened. Her face was full of anxiety, "John, have you bad news? Is something wrong? What's the matter?"

He stared at her. Her hair was white. She was slender as a reed. In her hand she was holding her spectacles. She had been reading, he supposed. Always reading.

"Are you just about to go out?" he asked her because her skirt was full-length to the ground, and her blouse seemed to have overlays of filmy lace.

"No, I am sitting by the fire. Is it my long skirt?" She smiled, "Clothes from the Iveagh Market."

Her smile may have been intended to take the barb out of the idea of second-hand clothes; he saw it as more of the usual provocation. His manner roughened, "You intend for me to stand out here all night?"

She seemed to hover with uncertainty. It felt an age until she stood back and he walked in. She locked the door, "It is a very old door, it could blow open." He liked the door being locked. He liked hanging up his coat on a rack beside her corduroy jacket.

She led the way into a sitting-room at the end of the hall. He did not like to stare around. He scarcely needed to. The room was familiar, evocative of some other sitting-room she had created in the dim past. In their first home? No, more likely the third...the one overlooking the harbour at Coliemore. She had liked that house. Suddenly he remembered the tears she had shed when he told her he was selling it. He had completely forgotten the tears. But he had got a great figure for that house. It had set him up.

He sat in the chair to one side of the fire. It was comfortable.

"What happened to your hair?" he asked.

"I let it go. What you might call 'an economy measure.'" She had not stressed the "you" but they were words he used habitually. He was not going to pursue that bait. All this was her idea, not his. And then he pursued it, "You are very thin. Another economy measure?"

Now she smiled in the old way, "No—just the fashion."

They sat looking into the fire. He could not think of a good opening phrase. Now he wished he had brought the flowers. Behind her armchair there was a stand of flowers. He was not sure if they were real. Quite a bouquet if they were. She used to make silk flowers and sell them. He had put a stop to that. Selling home-made produce was very demeaning to him. They weren't peasants, after all.

"Do you see much of the family?" he asked. She looked surprised as if he should know what the family did with their spare time.

"Occasionally," she replied, "I do not encourage them. There is one who has never come at all."

That would be the one he was stuck with, John knew. The bucko who made it his business to air his disapproval of deserting wives on every possible occasion—who had insistently put John on his mettle against this visit. At first it had looked like much-needed supportive loyalty but latterly it had revealed itself as self-directed righteousness.

"I wonder why you don't encourage them," he began but he knew the answer...it would be like leaching away his supporters. Supporters? He was more alone than she was.

"Why did you come, John?" Her voice was free from any emotion. "Why now? It has been a year."

He wanted to say that he came because he could not stay away. When his anger had drained out of him, he simply wanted her back—no matter what.

But he was damned if he was going to say those words. Not in a thousand years was he going to say them. Chasing after her. A man had his pride.

"I did not know your address until recently." He had spotted a letter in a daughter's open handbag, and filched what he was too proud to ask.

"Does that answer my question, then, John?"

"I suppose it does," he said stubbornly. The sense of being thwarted had begun to build up in him as it always did. Questions. Strings of bloody questions. Didn't she know all the things that were milling around in his mind? Didn't she know that if he didn't give a tinker's curse about her, he wouldn't be here? He wouldn't have come. He had done nothing but think about her for the last six months. More than six months. The anger hadn't lasted. Well, it had but the loneliness was worse. And all the damned, blasted, footling things you had to do for yourself without a woman. The daughters had not stayed long to help their poor bereaved father. Yes, bereaved was the word. He might as well be a widower. Into a flat in town with the daughters as fast as their legs would carry them.

He looked across at her. Her face was very still. Oh yes, she knew every thought he had in his head and a whole lot he never had. She could well look smug.

"Do you miss the golf?" he asked. She shook her head, smiling.

"Pity not to keep it up. You were good. You had the makings."

Her incredulous look held all the memories of all the frustrating games when he had told her she could do nothing right with a golf-club. "Throw your hat at it!" he used to roar with vexation. Now he remembered she had thrown his favourite five iron into the stream, and marched off the links. And that day, they were in a foursome. The humiliation of it. Still, she was only a woman. There was a lot to be said for keeping women out of golf clubs. They should have their own clubs—for women only—for God's sake. He opened his mouth to voice this bright idea. He abandoned the effort.

"I nearly got lost coming here." He had no notion he was going to complain and then he continued complaining. "This is a bit of a god-forsaken place you're living in, isn't it?"

She had a way of raising her eyes to him, a kind of deliberation otherwise unusual in her. And her voice was deeper than he remembered. "I like it," she said. The depth of her voice conveyed more than liking. There was contentment, security in the voice.

"Oh well, I meant old-fashioned," he said.

She shrugged in agreement. "The so-called conveniences are very old-fashioned."

"Hasn't the landlord renovated them?" he asked, indignant on her behalf.

"Money was never spent on these houses since they were built. I suppose Dean Swift kept his carriage horses here when the Cathedral was surrounded by fields."

He was always uneasy when she began to talk of historical Dublin and the characters who lived in it. Old Dublin, she called it. That was her sort of interest. A bit pretentious, he thought. As if the slums of Dublin contained the relics of the old aristocracy.

"My great-grandmother lived in this street when

she was a little girl. Her neighbours were the Sadleir family. They were artists."

"I felt you were going to tell me that," he said drily. "Well, my parents came up to Dublin from the midlands—from farms."

She was looking at him again in that contemplative way.

"And they despised Dublin," he added for good measure, "They despised Dublin for the slums."

"Poor old dirty Dublin," she murmured softly.

This conversation was killing him. It was not at all what he had, as he now realised, been hoping for. It was like all the scratchy conversations they used to have. Conversations to prove their absolute lack of interest in each other's interest. Conversations that were sparring matches and ended in rows. And the rows put a stop to conversation, or communication as she called it, for days and sometimes weeks of blanket silence.

Now they were staring into the fire again. He wished he had brought the flowers. Maybe compromised her into a bit of friendliness. He could have brought a bottle of wine. She liked wine.

"Would you like to come out and have a few drinks?" He fancied his manner to be full of bonhomie, "Maybe sample one of the Old Dublin hostelries?"

She lowered her head to smile. She has gone very secretive, he thought. "Thank you, no. I would not want to go out."

She stood up to take a bottle and a glass from a small, shabby davenport. More old stuff from the Iveagh Market, he thought. He could not abide shabby, worn-out antiques. Empty pretensions.

She put the bottle on a low table beside his chair. "Do you need water?" she asked politely.

He did not want her to leave the room, to go away from his sight. "I'll drink it neat," he said, adding inwardly, "What there is of it." He wondered who had drunk the rest of her whiskey or indeed how did she come to have a bottle of whiskey? He was about to ask her could she afford to be buying bottles of Jameson? He was also about to criticise the way she was poking at the fire. She never did learn how to fix a fire with maximum efficiency.

He concentrated his mind on pouring the drink. A sudden practical fact had occurred to him: he was a visitor here. Merely a visitor.

"Do you have many visitors?" he enquired.

"Apart from the family, you mean? No, not really. I do not bother."

He wondered what she did all day. "You must miss the house? The garden?"

She shook her head and then she laughed, "You know perfectly well, John, I was not interested in housework—ever!"

"You loved cooking," he said defensively.

She looked surprised, "Did I?" Would he tell her how much he missed her cooking? Especially the savoury smell of it wafting around? How he had discovered in himself absolute laziness where eating was concerned—if he had to cook it! Open a tin, or make a ham sandwich, was the total extent of his culinary knowledge. "I suppose the girls have told you that I am the world's worst cook?"

Her surprise deepened, "The girls? Oh no, their interest is negative unless it is a slimming diet or maybe a dinner in the Shelbourne."

"Isn't it well for them that can afford the Shelbourne."

"I was not too serious," she said in her low tone, "but they did take me there to dinner on my birthday."

He supposed that was fair enough—once you accepted the fact that it was their birthday-mother who had deserted the family home. The father who had stuck to his post had never been invited to dinner in the Shelbourne, birthday or no birthday. He checked this line of reasoning with what he thought was a change of subject, "Johnny and his girl-friend usually cook on the weekend. She has a rare lot to learn—although she fancies herself as a cordon blue or something—took lessons, she says. They were under the impression that when they cooked, yours truly would do the wash-up! I soon let them know they had another guess coming! Then the girl (I forget her name, Angela or something) was making plans to install a dishwashing machine. Next thing, she would be installing herself to use the machine!"

"A dishwashing machine sounds marvellous," she murmured.

He drained his whiskey glass, "When that young woman gets Johnny to the altar, she will be cooking in her own kitchen—a considerable distance from mine, I can tell you."

"Have you told Johnny?"

"In no uncertain terms, I assure you."

She seemed a little troubled, "I know Johnny has expectations." She raised her eyes to him thoughtfully, "Don't you like Johnny's fiancée?"

"I don't like her enough to install her in my kitchen where I would install a wife."

Now his tongue had run away with him. She would think that sounded brutal. It was reminiscent of the things she used to object to. It didn't sound the way he meant, it sounded the way he didn't mean it to—oh hell, it always sounded wrong when he began to communicate. He hated that word communicate, cause of all the trouble. How the hell did they get on to cooking? Wives, she had told him often enough, need to be valued above and beyond their menial tasks. He supposed cooking was menial in wives' eyes? Come to think of it, weren't all menial tasks done by electric gadgets nowadays? It was many a long day since he had seen a woman scrubbing doorsteps. His mother used to scrub their doorstep every morning and he often admired the adroit way his father stepped over her bowed back, on his way to work.

"Winter or summer," John said inconsequentially, "My father left the house at seven-thirty a.m.!"

Out of the corner of his eye, he saw her taking a peep at her wrist-watch. He settled himself deeply into the chair. It had taken him many, many weeks to work up a head of steam for this visit. So far, he hadn't got much out of it. So far.

"I got to thinking about you," he said importantly. All she replied was a quiet "oh." Anyone else, any ordinary woman, would have been very interested and responsive, would surely have asked, "Oh, in what way?" He persevered doggedly, "Thinking were you fixed up—comfortable? Had you got your needs?"

She made no reply. Her white hair gleamed like

silver in the firelight. The room was almost in darkness. For a fleeting moment, he thought of kneeling by her chair. He knew her—she would say it was the whiskey. Oh, she could be very scathing about the effects of drink but she never stopped to think how whiskey gave a man a bit of courage, helped his tongue to loosen. Strangely enough, since she went away, he seemed to have cut down on the binges. Or was it that he didn't notice?

She switched on a rosy standard lamp. Now she drew the heavy curtains.

"I could make you a cup of tea," she was courtesy itself if courtesy can be totally devoid of warmth.

"Don't put yourself to any trouble on my account," he replied in the curt, brisk tone of one who says, Two can play at that game.

Her voice softened. "I usually have a cup of tea at this time. See, I have the electric kettle here, and all I need. Otherwise, I should have to go down to the basement. That is where the kitchen is."

"Surely to God, your landlord ought to spend a few thousand on these ramshackles?"

"It is fine. I like it," her voice was even, "and if you want to avail of the usual places, there is a light on the stairs."

"Thank you," he said, adding jocosely, "I thought you would never ask!" but this did not raise a smile; she busied herself with the kettle.

She was a bloody stupid woman and obstinate. She knew perfectly well that he would spend the money to improve the place. On second thoughts, spending money on rented accommodation was a mug's game. And for what? To make her more comfortable in a home that wasn't her right home?

The conveniences were somewhat pretentious, as it turned out. Quite obviously she had spent a fair bit on replacements and paint. It was elegant, in fact.

When he came back, he hesitated to praise the set-up. It could sound patronising. She never had liked to be patronised; she bridled—although, in his view, the idea of his patronising her was all in her imagination. Like a lot of other things. She had a whale of an imagination at times.

She had set out some cups and biscuits. The room was cosy and welcoming. She always had a special knack with a room. He never could get the room at home to look even comfortable nowadays. He usually took one look at it, and hared off to his local. There was always a good log fire blazing away in the pub. The landlady always gave him a very warm-hearted greeting, making it sound special. She was a grand woman, to be sure, but the way she bestowed her capacious bosom up on the counter repelled him a little. Someone should tell her. On the other hand, some there would say it was part of her charm.

"I should have insisted on taking you out for a few jars," he said.

She glanced again at her watch. His heart lurched with expectation. Her deep voice was satin-smooth when she spoke, "John, you will still have time for a few quick ones with Mrs Tubbs!"

"You never lost it, did you!" But, in truth, the bitter sting he remembered in her voice was not there anymore. She was smiling a little wearily.

"You are laughing now," he growled at her, "but it might interest you to know that I am a rare enough client in Tubbs's these days."

It did not interest her. She did not reply. She was

staring into the fire again, crouching a little lower in her chair, seeming smaller than of old. He felt he could take her in his arms, she looked defenceless. The words that kept on coming into his mind would surely come to his lips if he could go down beside her chair. I need you. I need you. Oh if you could only know how much I need you…I…

"Did you have enough tea?" She was moving the cups and the teapot almost as if she had read his thoughts. She was clearing the space between their armchairs as if to set the scene. She put some coal on the fire, and brushed the hearth-dust inwards. There was an overpowering familiarity in her quiet movements, a familiarity utterly dear to him. He imagined a faint perfume from the rustle of her clothes.

"You are still wearing my rings, I see," he said. She held out her hands, the rings sparkling in the firelight. "Of course!" she said, "I would be lonely without them—I love my engagement ring, although it fulfilled its promise—opals for tears." She kissed the ring gently.

May I kiss your ring, too, please let me. But the words would not come out. Let me kiss your hand—just that and then I'll go, if I must. Oh please listen to me…I want to tell you…

"And of course I wear my Spanish wedding-ring," she said, "Hard to believe we are twenty-five years married. It is always much admired." She turned it on her finger, herself admiring it.

What's the good, he thought despairingly. I can't. She sits there as cool as a breeze. I dare not risk refusal. I have been through so much. She will have to make the move. She knows how I feel. She knows all the words. A man has got only his pride—and God knows she had dragged that in the mud. The humiliation she has put me through, there's no end to it. Now he imagined his big, unwieldy frame struggling to the floor. He would seize her hands, she would snatch them away. He would put his arms around her and she would press back from him. He would almost kiss and she would twist her mouth from his.

She had gone out into the hall, passing close to his chair. Oh God, how much he needed her...day after day, night after night, longing to wake up from the nightmare of loneliness, longing to find her in the garden kneeling and smiling in the springtime discovery of some little green shoot and looking up at him as she used to long ago.

She had brought in his coat from the hall. Standing proudly, her arms stretched high, she was holding the coat up for him. It was a solemn gesture that perceived, and denied, the reason behind this visit. To the woman who wore his rings of fealty, he was merely a relative with whom she had shared her fireside and her pot of tea. The uninvited guest was ushered out, the door was firmly closed, the fanlight darkened.

In the street, a surge of anger stormed through him in a way he scarcely recognised. He, who had always known himself for a calm man, a fair man, a man given to quiet reason, felt himself exploding into a hundred expletives of ungrateful bitches and damned naggers and worse. His teeth gritted so he almost choked. In blind rage, he fumbled to open the car door and he crammed into the seat as he might have crushed onto a body and he rammed in the starter-key as he might have forced himself into…no, no, it was not like that. For a moment, the violence of his wrath repelled him. It was not only, not just only, that he wanted her, he needed her, he needed her—the delicate turn of her neck as she lifted her eyes to him. Surely she had been telling him something in that long contemplative look. The loneliness of it? The sadness of it?

Then his anger returned. The repudiation of him and his lawful desires, that's what her wary look meant. Yes, lawful. She was still his wife, he had his rights. Crawl to her? Was that her idea? By God, that would be the day!

Furiously he jerked the car from the kerb onto the road, glancing from habit into his rear-view mirror. Then he slammed down the brake. Through the mirror he saw a car pulling into the position he had vacated, under the street-lamp. He watched.

A burly fellow got out of the car. From the boot he took two suitcases and put them down at the door of the house from which John Blane had been banished. From the inside of the car, he brought out some parcels. Then he went about carefully locking up the car, and testing to be sure it was locked.

So that was it! The virtuous wife had a lover! John Blane's passionate grief at expulsion went out like a tidal wave and gushed back in a torrent of righteous indignation. A lover! That explained everything. The secretive looks. A kept woman, else how could she afford to live? Second-hand clothes from the Iveagh Market? Oh sure! Like lacy blouses, for instance? She didn't encourage visitors—you bet she didn't! Not even a bona fide husband. Help him into his coat. Hurry him out the door. The half-empty whiskey bottle? There's the vital clue. Your man must have his drop of malt to keep his strength up. By God, he is going to need his strength when John Blane gets to him!

The man was hesitating at the door. Narrowly, cunningly, John watched him, his hands gripping the steering-wheel as if to wrench it from its socket and use it as a lethal weapon. Just give the bastard time to get inside, get sitting at that glowing fire, get planning their night ahead. Just the bare time and then, by Almighty God, that rickety old door will be burst in on them. No! Just the bare time for that bastard to hang his coat on that bloody rack!

The man was picking up his suitcases. He was crossing the street to the house directly opposite. He rapped resoundingly on the door-knocker. The fanlight filled with light, the door was flung open. Loud Dublin voices welcomed in the burly traveller.

Let Me Say the Words

B arry was jubilant. He settled his mother into the car. She could see the completely happy smile on his handsome face as he got in behind the wheel. He had taken her quietness for granted. She had always been quiet. That her manner was evasive, he was too contentedly preoccupied to notice.

The drive home from the pre-wedding reception in the girl's home would take no more than half an hour. There was time to show interest and enthusiasm.

"That was a lovely evening, Barry," his mother said. "You are going to be very happy. Eleanor is a beautiful girl."

"Sure, Mum! I knew you would go mad about Eleanor! I couldn't wait for you to meet her."

"And what a charming family, Barry. Her mother looks so young. So full of life, don't you think?"

"She's okay," Barry laughed, "when she's had a good few gins."

"Barry," murmured his mother, a little shocked.

"But I like Eleanor's dad," Barry said, unabashed. "I like him a lot. When Eleanor wrote to me that he was prepared to take me into the business—sight unseen as I was still in the States—I pictured some doddery old guy ready to retire. But he's just great.

He's a fantastic golfer, did you know?"

"Really. Yes, I thought he was very nice." She pressed on, "You got lovely wedding presents, Barry."

Barry was delighted with her praise. "Sure did! Did you see the cutlery I got from the firm, all the staff in Holroyds? All the way from Boston. Fantastic stuff! And buckets of it! Eleanor is going to have dinner parties. She says that you and my dad along with her parents are going to be our very first guests. Eleanor is mad keen on the idea of dinner parties. Did she show you the red wallpaper for the lounge. She was showing it to everyone. And she has her eye on red leather chairs. Did you notice the electric fire like a big medieval brazier. It has built-in bookcases and a bronze cowl. Did you notice it, Mum? Isn't it fantastic? Eleanor got her Aunt Clare to give us that. The old Aunt is loaded, and she adores Eleanor."

"Yes, I thought that was lovely," his mother lied, "And it will look good with books..."

Barry burst out laughing. "That's the gas of it! We haven't got a book between us. Only my textbooks, and a lot of them were second-hand to start with. Eleanor hasn't read a book since she left school. She hates reading!"

"Oh, and what does she like doing?"

"You know what," replied Barry, glancing around smilingly. "She is crazy about cooking. Chinese food and all the trimmings. And she loves travelling. And swimming. And horses. And, oh yes, pub-crawling! Oh, no, Mum—not serious drinking. Just messing about in pubs—meeting the old gang—hers and mine. The Irish pubs in Boston are all right, but there is nothing to come up to a Dublin pub."

His mother did not care for this casual attitude to drinking. She put in an advisory word. "I am sure you both look forward to settling down, Barry?"

"Sure! Sure! All in good time, Mum. Eleanor is keeping on the boutique. I told you, on the phone, about her little shop, didn't I, Mum? In fact, she is going to expand. She has marvellous ideas. She has all her friends competing with names for the new front. She is getting some sign-writer guy to do it. She thinks "ELEANORA" very elegant. You know, when I met her first I thought she was the original dumb blonde! Anything but! She's got real drive."

His mother looked at him with love. His admiration for his bride-to-be was very moving. She touched his hand on the steering-wheel. "I am so glad for you. Barry May you never have a single worry."

"I never do worry, Mum. I'm lucky. I had a fantastic ten years in the States. *You* know that, everything went right for me. And meeting Eleanor was a chance in a million—a girl from Dublin—and she was only there for a month on a holiday. She wouldn't want to live there—not with all her family here. Neither of us is much good with the letter-writing. The phone bills were horrific—and in the middle of the night! Then her dad wrote, offering me the job—next year there will be a partnership—probably junior, but what the hell—bob's yer uncle as Dad used to say. And Mum, what about Dad? You're sure he will be at the wedding on Tuesday? He's okay isn't he?"

His mother was hesitant. "Well, Barry, it's like this. He had a touch of rheumatism, er, lately...and he...really..."

Barry was alarmed. "Are you holding something from me, Mum? He's not crippled with it, is he? He is well, isn't he?"

"Fairly well, darling. It is just…"

"But able to walk okay, isn't he?" Barry insisted.

"Fairly well, darling. That is, he can walk…oh, yes…"

Barry interrupted her. "I suppose you have guessed that I am a bit miffed at not being invited home for the few days before the wedding? I don't know what excuse Eleanor made to her mother. It looked a bit down-market."

"Barry, I am sorry…I…"

"No, Mum, I am sure it is not your fault. I don't blame you, you always did everything you could to keep the peace. And I suppose I was a bit of a handful when I was nineteen."

"At nineteen, one doesn't have much sense," his mother's quiet voice was faintly reassuring.

"Sure, Mum. I remember you said that at the time. But after all, it was costing Dad a stack to keep me in College. His business wasn't going well. It was only after he ordered me out of the house that I heard that he had to let staff go. I bet he never got such good chaps as those again. Do you remember Freddy? Freddy Williams? He told me about Dad's losses."

"Freddy Williams is back," his mother said. "He is foreman now." She knew little enough about her husband's business, but it seemed to have recovered.

"Oh good!" Barry said. "That means everything is all right."

He pulled the car into the side and rolled down the window. He stared up at the house. "Here we are, Mum. Home sweet home. And there's a light on in the front window. I'll come in with you. I have always wanted to tell Dad that I am sorry."

Her voice was troubled, "Sorry?"

"Sure!" replied Barry warmly."I have often thought of that night. I came in drunk...oh, I was drunk alright...blotto...paralytic. Only the previous day, he had given me fifty quid. Fifty quid in brand-new fivers. You never knew that, did you, Mum? Fifty quid because I owed bits of money all over the place. I was a right little tyke and he knew it."

"You were only a child." But now her voice lacked conviction.

"Some child!" Barry laughed at her innocence. "Some child. I took a street-woman out on that fifty quid—what the lads called a 'Wan.'"

He had distressed, and embarrassed, his mother. She turned on him as if imploring. "I could not believe that, Barry."

"Sure you can believe it, Mum. He never told you? I'm not exactly proud of that night. The wan got thirty out of the fifty. And when I had paid her I didn't know what to do next. So she took me to a pub in Liffey Street, and the other twenty went on drink. She introduced me to her friends there as a big spender. Some high livin'! She disappeared—she hooked off with some older guy—and I staggered home. Not a quid left of my father's hard-earned fifty! And was I ever drunk!"

"I had better go in now, Barry."

Barry was contrite. "Now I've upset you. I am sorry, Mum. That was all so long ago. It is like another world, the distant past. Didn't I tell you, in a letter, how sorry I was for all the trouble I had been—going out with the lads, failing exams. I know you used to stick up for me, Mum. Was it twice I wrote to Dad? He never answered. But your letters were a life-line. I read somewhere that women find it easier to write letters than men…"

His mother was trying to open the car door. "Wait, Mum, I'll come around and open the door. I'll come in with you."

His mother gripped his arm. "No, Barry. No!"

"Why, Mum?"

She was distraught. "I should like to prepare the, er, ground. I mean, to talk about… I mean to, er, tell him…well, to say…"

"To say what?" Barry was worried by his mother's flustered nervousness. His memory was of her calm and kindly dignity. "Are you all right, Mum? Dad knows I am back, doesn't he? He knows I am to be married on Tuesday? But sure of course he does—the marvellous present you gave us is from both of you. From both of you with all your love—Eleanor said we will treasure the card for ever, no one else thought of adding their love in as well. I am coming in with you. I would like to see him before the wedding—tell him about my job and all. And, of course, he has to meet Eleanor. I invented all sorts of important business engagements for his absence today—although I did not know until you told me that he still has the business. Eleanor says…"

"You have told Eleanor…?"

"That Dad kicked me out? No fear! It is not important. That is all over. Who knew anyway? You warned me yourself, Mum, not to go blabbing my mouth off to the relations in Boston. Things happened so fast going to the States and all, I hadn't time to think. Well, I had, but it is not important now."

"Barry, give me a little time to talk to him—please, Barry." She was almost in tears.

"Okay, okay, Mum—sure I will. Don't be upset. But he knows about me, doesn't he? About getting married? I thought he would have phoned when he couldn't come today. He is okay? Mum, is he okay?"

His mother began to plead now that she was sure she had gained time. "You know how he is, Barry. Never very keen on parties, or...or ceremonies. Yes, you know, not keen on dressing up, late nights, that sort of thing. You remember, Barry? Just give me a little time...please..."

"Sure, Mum, sure. If that's how he is now. You have your little chat and I'll ring you later." He looked at his wrist-watch, "Say about nine?"

"Yes, nine. No, no, half-past nine."

"Sure, even better. Nine-thirty. That will not be too late to bring Eleanor. Okay, Mum ? See you later, then."

Barry drove off, bipping the car-horn cheerfully.

When the woman opened the hall door, the house was filled with music. Through the glass panelling she could see her husband sitting in his accustomed place. He was watching television on which, apparently, there was a symphony concert. He gave no indication of hearing the hall door, and she could not make herself go into the room.

She went into the kitchen to prepare a supper-tray. Nervously, she clattered the cups onto the saucers. In her orderly kitchen, suddenly there were things she could not find. At last, holding the tray and practising a smile, she tried the words: "Barry is going to be married on Tuesday." Her voice came out in a strangled whisper.

Shakily she set the tray down. Then she tried again: "Barry is back. He is to be married on Tuesday." There was no sound, and tears clouded her vision. She took a drink of water. She splashed her face. Standing or sitting, her legs trembled. Oh God, she whispered, let me say the words. Please God, let me say the words.

With a tremendous effort, she took up the tray and went into the room. She poured out the tea, placed his cup on a low table near him, then she sat in her usual place. Her husband picked up his cup without acknowledging her presence. She turned towards him and tried to make herself speak. The only sound was the music pouring from the television. Suddenly, terrified that she might scream, she hurried from the room and up the stairs to her bedroom

When she shut the door and pressed her back to it, her throat seemed to open and breathe. She spoke aloud. "It is true, then, I am dumb in his presence. The years of silence have done this. Dumb when I come into his presence. Dumb is a hateful word but I have made it so. When he enters the house my spirit takes refuge in a desert where dumb and deaf ghosts mime at household chores. Dumb now for years. I tried. I tried. I could not speak."

She sat down at her mirror. Now I will practise, she thought: Barry has come back. He is engaged to a pretty girl. He wants you, no, he wants us to come to his wedding. Barry wants to say he is sorry.

SORRY. SORRY. SORRY. The word crashed against the mirror, splintering it into a hundred pictures of her husband and of herself. She is standing in the hall holding a letter in her hand. It is for him.

"This came for you today. It is a letter from Barry."

"What does he want?"

"It is for you. I didn't open it."

"Well, open it now. Read it while I eat. I have to hurry back."

"No, you read it. It is addressed to you."

"It took him six months to write it. It is six months?"

"Seven months."

"Ho! Seven—and a few days and a few hours, I suppose."

"Won't you take it, at least?"

"Oh, shove it up there. I'm in a hurry."

"You were always in a hurry where Barry was concerned."

"Meaning what?"

"Always your business first. Never a father for a son."

"Your little ewe-lamb never went short, did he?"

"You think money is everything."

"I can think of a good answer to that, but I am in a hurry. May I have my dinner, please?"

"Get your own dinner."

Smothering a word he puts back on his coat and slams out the door.

Staring through her tears at the mirror, feeling a guilt she was reluctant to admit...the camera of memory was inexorable:

Her husband surveying the table. "Set for one? Aren't you going to join me?"

"No, I am busy."

"You are only writing a letter."

"I must catch the post."

"What special post when the letter is to America?"

They glare at each other.

"It is to America, isn't it?"

"Yes," she snaps and turns her back on him.

"Look," he begins softly. She does not answer. He tries again, louder: *"Look, it is nearly two years since he went. By all accounts he is doing all right."*

"By whose account? I have not said anything."

"No, but if he wanted help—you would, quick enough."

"Ask you? Never!"

"Here we go again. All I wanted to say was… couldn't we forget the whole thing? Now wait. Let me speak."

"Forget the whole thing? You say that? You, who kicked him out of this room, out through the hall door, down the steps. You."

"Yes, I know, but that's two years ago. I want to forget…"

"Forget!" She screams and, screaming, she races upstairs to lock herself in her bedroom.

That was a long time ago, she told the mirror. Tonight he does not follow me, nor any night now. That night he followed her. He pounded on the door, and shouted himself hoarse.

"Listen to me, can't you! You're just being silly. You can't build your life on a nineteen-year-old kid kicking over the traces. He's young. He'll survive. What about me? Don't you have a duty towards me? Hasn't this bloody argument gone on long enough! Hasn't it."

He paused and listened. She was crying.

"Look, stop bawling and.we'll bury the hatchet. Do you hear me? What good is bawling? You're always bawling. Come on out and stop being silly. Your son isn't the only thing in the world. Look, listen to me, will you?"

He racks his brain for something plausible to say. Nothing comes.

"Look, I tell you what. Come on out and we'll go out for a jar! It'll be like old times. Come on. Do you hear me?"

Slowly the woman took off her coat. Opening the wardrobe to hang up the coat, she saw the new outfit she had bought for Barry's wedding. The thought came to her to dress herself for the wedding. To walk into the room below, bedecked in her new finery, her face made up, her hair fluffed out under the new hat. Her new hat was just the sort of hat that her husband used to admire on her years ago, a tiny bandeau of net and rosebuds. He must surely notice her when she walked into the room. He must look up at her, and that would give her the courage to say the words.

Quickly she attended to her face. She put on the new shoes, and slipped the dainty dress into place. Her hair had been set for the party, it needed only the flick of a brush. The matching jacket was next. She went to the mirror to see the effect.

I feel grotesque doing this, she thought. He will think I have gone crazy if I cannot speak immediately to explain. The mirrored camera gave her back another picture of the many, many times he had tried to win her over: *"What sort of a screwball are you? Are you going to lock yourself into that room forever. Are you trying to drive yourself nutty? Can you hear me? Why can't you answer me? Come on out and we'll go up to the pub. You used to like that. We'll have a few jars. Wouldn't a whacker of brandy do you good? Jeez, how can you hear me if you won't stop snivelling? Are you coming out? If you won't come out, I'll go without*

97

you—do you hear me! Open the door, can't you"

He crashed on the door with his fists. Suddenly, he cooled down. *"To hell with you,"* he said, *"I'm going out and if you don't stop being silly and start being sensible, I am staying out. You can drive yourself mad but you are not going to drive me mad."* After that night, he ceased to plead, and that was years ago.

The woman turned her back to the mirror. The pictures were gone, giving place to sober thought. In the beginning, he had rolled in when the bars closed. There came nights when he did not return at all. He was either too drunk to drive home, or he found solace in some other place. The household cheque was left on the mantelpiece. The silence was never broken. The heavy drinking gradually ceased; he resumed his old habit of regular hours. It became apparent that his business worries were over. He bought a new car, he bought a colour television. He looked impressive. He had even begun to put on a little weight. He lived in his own house like a tame bachelor, a star boarder.

I will go down. I will, she told herself.

The telephone began to ring in the hall. Her husband would let it ring, she was always the one to answer the phone. She dabbed at her face with the powder-puff, looking around for the gay little hat to complete her outfit. The hat-box was still on top of the wardrobe.

The telephone began to sound impatient.

Hastily she pulled a chair over to the high old-fashioned wardrobe and stepping up, she reached for the box. The chair was toppling, she grabbed blindly for support.

The tremendous crash of the falling wardrobe reverberated in the house.

As the man rushed through the hall, he snatched up the telephone, "Excuse me one moment. I think there has been an accident."

A Kind of Comfort

Cassy read the death notice through again, very carefully. Then the phone rang. She rushed to answer, it could be Robert. Oh, let it be Robert!

"It's only me." It was his sister, Sadie, "I suppose you saw the notice?"

"I am just reading it—I do get the daily paper, you know!" Cassy checked the acid note in her voice. If she were to go for the funeral, she would have to ask Sadie to take the dogs, and her sister's husband did not like dogs.

"It is a great shock," she told her sister in quite another voice, "I did not know Louise was sick."

"Do you suppose she had a heart attack? Are you going to ring him? You've been out of touch lately, haven't you? Will you go down for the funeral?"

Cassy thought her sister was growing daily more like their dead mother, always the litany of questions. She never could abide Sadie's inquisitive bossy manner and she could not stand Sadie's husband but neither could she do without them.

"I did not go down in the summer. You may remember I had to..." Cassy began.

"I thought they didn't invite you last summer?"

The trouble with Sadie was her inconvenient memory. One should not confide in her. Last summer was the first summer no invitation had come for the annual month in Kerry with Robert and Louise. There was no reason given and no letters exchanged. The usual Christmas card was their response to Cassy's long and affectionate Christmas letter.

"What did you say?" Cassy asked in answer to the questions still running on.

"I said are you going to brush up your typing skills? Didn't the dead wife do all his typing? Maybe you would like a job in your old age?"

"Honestly, Sadie, will you ever give up? I am just taking in the fact that Robert's wife is dead. Louise was my friend."

"Louise! Are you saying now that you haven't fancied Robert for the last twenty years? Why do you buy all his boring books? Do you ever read them?"

"Of course I read them!" Sadie knew perfectly well that Cassy would need a string of degrees as a foundation for reading Robert's books.

"Are you going up for the funeral? Are you asking us to take the dogs? Will you do it in one day? Would it be over a hundred miles there and back?"

Suddenly Cassy's mind snapped like a camera. It opened to light the path to a different future. It shut on the necessity of enduring Sadie for ever.

"Yes!" she said distinctly, "I will drive down tonight when I have taken the dogs to the kennels. And now may I ring you later, I have other business." Sadie would not forgive that in a hurry, but maybe—just maybe—Cassy would not have to care.

Sadie was back on the line again. She was not one

to give up easily. "Look, Cassy, don't go down there making a fool of yourself. You know you were always a right idiot where Louise was concerned. Yes, I know she is dead and I shouldn't speak ill of the dead. She was a blood-sucker and I have no reason to think he is any different. No, listen to me, Cassy, I feel responsible for you. Yes, I know you are not a child, but in a way you are. No, listen, I know the world better than you…"

Cassy replaced the receiver. Sadie could go on all day. Responsible for her? Responsible for a forty-year-old? She waited for the querulous sound of Sadie's voice to die out of her ears. Then she phoned the kennels. No problem, they would send the man to collect the dogs before midday. The kennels were expensive, but in a warmly unthrifty frame of mind, in the circumstances, Cassy felt the expense could go hang.

She dusted her best and nicest travel-bag and sat down in her bedroom to consider a choice of clothes. It was a long way to go for a funeral, she would have to stay overnight. She was sure Robert would offer her the hospitality of his home. Robert's hospitality was legendary, even if she herself had not experienced it since last summer twelve-months. It was almost two years since she had seen him, and Louise of course…she wondered how long Louise was ill, or was it sudden? Well, she would soon know. She pictured Robert taking her hands in his, and sadly relating the history of Louise's sickness. Robert had often held Cassy's hands in his, telling her of his youthful struggles when he first began to write—yes, often, during the month's holiday at Caragh Lake where she had gone to them each July for twenty years. Twenty years made hundreds of times of holding hands and turning lovely compliments. What pretty hair you have, Cassy! He had said that nearly every year. And how quick you are—that too. Cassy would rush through the breakfast dishes and the dinner preparations and the bed-making and the tidying-up so as to be free for the few hours when Louise was busy with the day's correspondence. Then Robert would drive Cassy into Killorglin with Louise's shopping list. Sometimes there was no shopping list. Robert would take out the boat and they would drift across the lake. Perhaps, out of sight of the bungalow, he would light cigarettes for both of them. "This is idyllic," he would say, "just you and I in the wilderness." Cassy could not remember what poetical reply she made, he always leaned forward and laughed, and her heart would jump sideways. She knew she was waiting for the hour, for the year, when he would kiss her. Walking up from the lake, under the trees, he caressed her bare arm with an intensity that promised more. One starry night in the last summer she was there, the three of them had walked slowly along the lake shore. Robert had held each of them closely to him as they walked. His fingers had touched her breast with infinite tenderness. It was devastating for a woman who had never known the searching fingers of a lover. Suddenly Louise had pleaded tiredness, and the wonderful night was over.

Louise was tired quite often. Often, too, she protested at the endless stream of visitors that came to Robert's summer lodge. She was very glad of Cassy's help in the house. There were days when the phone never stopped ringing and Robert was too occupied with guests. Louise and Robert told her, constantly, how good she was. Cassy always smilingly reminded them that Louise was her oldest friend, they had been friends all through their schooldays. Robert used to say what a shame Cassy had never married, how could such a treasure go unclaimed, and he would tease her when she blushed with pleasure. Louise knew that Cassy had sacrificed her life for her parents in their long years of poor health. Now they, too, were gone. All she had to remember them were her mother's two ageing dogs—and, of course, the family home that was so expensive to run and heat nowadays.

Cassy had arranged all her newest and nicest underwear on her bed. Now she inspected the colourful assortment. She selected the most filmy and laciest of the nightdresses, with a négligé of rose silk embroidered with rosebuds. She folded in tissue paper her best suit, a suitable navy, with a dark blue silk blouse, and matching shoes and gloves. She paused a long time over the choice of perfume. Then she considered earrings, holding them to her ear at the mirror. She was the same age as the dead Louise, but she persuaded herself she had always looked younger. Robert was at least ten years older, maybe even more? Instinctively, she thought it important to look young and healthy at this funeral—and attractive, of course. Looks were surely more important than years.

Cassy set off in good time to arrive at Robert's home in the midlands in the late evening. If the hand of friendship should fail to draw her into the house and accommodate her for the night, then there would still be time to put up at the local hotel, go quietly to the funeral of her old school-friend and steal silently away. That, in fact, was not the scene Cassy began to anticipate as she drove carefully along the country roads. Robert's eyes would light up when he saw her, his deep cultured voice would warmly welcome her caring thoughtfulness in driving all that distance to honour his poor dead lady—laid out, no doubt, in some funeral parlour, and unable for once to terminate their cosy conversation. Indeed, when Cassy looked back on those sunlit days at Caragh Lake, Louise's shadow was forever falling across the grass.

She wondered again why Louise had not written to her for last summer. Robert and Louise had gone to Caragh Lake, Cassy had found that out easily enough. She supposed now that she should have written to them. Cassy had always been diffident with Louise since schooldays. Louise was the brilliant one, the ambitious social-climbing one. She was a beautiful woman. Cassy was too proud of Louise's friendship to risk losing it. To risk losing it? Or to risk losing access to Robert? Both really, thought Cassy, with an emotion she believed to be loyalty.

Cassy knew Robert's house was on the main road on the edge of the small provincial town. She recognised it easily from the many photographs she had seen in Louise's album. It was a house to be proud of, a country residence set among old trees and lawns, almost out of sight behind its ornate iron gates. Louise had told Cassy that she would like to live all the year round at Caragh Lake with just Cassy to help her. The expense of a maid and a char and a gardener were quite crippling, she often moaned. She never said these things in Robert's hearing. Robert adored his country home where he could receive colleagues from all over the world and cater for them in elegant comfort. At Caragh Lake, Louise often talked of all the exciting glamorous personalities who had stayed with them through the years, famous names that Cassy knew only from the newspapers. Once there had been a tentative suggestion that Cassy should come as a guest to Garlow Lodge, and be Louise's helper. Alas at that time, Cassy had to care for her mother after her father's death. Later, Cassy could have gone to Garlow Lodge. The suggestion had not been repeated. Now, of course, the road to helping Robert was unobstructed.

There were people out on the steps of the house as Cassy was driving up the avenue. Robert was bidding goodbye to callers. This was lucky, Cassy thought, she had been rather dreading having to knock on the door. He did not go in as she came up the steps, neither did he recognise her. He wore his deliberate air of abstracted absent-mindedness. Cassy remembered this look, it could be switched on for unwanted visitors, those Louise called "intruders."

Cassy was confident she was not an intruder—not for Robert.

"I'm Cassy," she said, "Cassy from Caragh Lake."

Very slowly his face cleared, and then more rapidly as if a sudden thought had dissolved the fog of recollection.

"Ah Cassy! But of course Cassy!" He took her hand and drew her in. "And you came all this way!

But how kind of you! But of course you were a very old friend of Louise."

"The oldest," Cassy smiled, feeling that now their special past would rush back to him, "we started school together on the same day."

"Ah yes indeed! And you were always her great friend." He was leading her along a hall, past rooms on either side and down some steps to a green baize door. Cassy was thinking that Louise lay in her coffin beyond this door—Louise beautiful as in life, covered with spring flowers...his dead wife, Louise.

The baize door led into a kitchen where a woman was busily occupied.

"Mrs MacNeill, this is Cassy. She has come to help you."

The woman straightened up, "Gee, that's good! Great! I seem to have made a zillion cups of tea! Hiya Cassy? Howya doin'? Grab an apron. Here's a knife. I got a cake just about mixed. There's all that bread to butter for sandwiches."

Cassy was taken aback. No one noticed that she was struck dumb. No one had mentioned death. This woman was either American or Australian, certainly not the local maid type of help that Cassy would have expected.

She turned to Robert. The door-bell was ringing. Robert disappeared through the baize door, shutting it firmly behind him.

"I drove a long way," Cassy said defensively as she tied on an apron.

"Is that right, eh?" responded the woman, not stopping to chat, "pull up the stool while you're working."

"I would like to wash my hands," Cassy said, putting a delicate hint in her voice.

"Oh sure! The loo is down the corridor, right by the back door. You'll find soap 'n stuff."

When Cassy returned to the kitchen, she set herself to the buttering of bread. After all, this was a house of death and it was traditional to prepare food for mourners. She had come, she told herself firmly, to help Robert through these few days, and further should he need her. She could not deny to herself that she had thought, if a little vaguely, to come into a position of organising staff. Now indeed she wondered at the strangeness of this household...none of the female help of whose wage-bill Louise used to complain to Cassy in their little private talks at Caragh Lake.

Mrs MacNeill came through the baize door, shouldering it open. She was carrying a big tray of glasses and empty bottles.

"Those guys have some capacity!" she laughed huskily. "We are running out of hard liquor. You got a car? I am sure the pubs are still open—are they ever shut! Would you? Some of the pubs have shops at the back. Hey, why don't I make a list? We need cooked ham, and any other cold meat that is not too mottled—a few pounds of each. Oh yes, more eggs and lettuce. Let's say four Irish and four Scotch. No, six of each and mixers." She had opened the fridge, and was studying the contents, "More milk, and butter. I have plenty of bread. How about biscuits? Yes, get half a dozen packets. While you do that, I'll finish the sandwiches, and my cake will be ready, just about."

Mrs MacNeill gave Cassy the list and ushered her

out the back door, "and best come in this way with the parcels."

The tradesmen's entrance, Cassy thought as she turned the key in her car. Thoroughly disgruntled, she realised she had not been given any money to buy the considerable list of drinks and groceries. Oh well, she reflected, this is all for Robert. She thought of her first sight of him this evening, as he stood out on his steps. He was a very handsome man. He looked now a little beyond middle age; and although his hair was white it was still crisp and groomed. Cassy was looking forward to the moment when they would be alone together. He would remember that she had not had the opportunity to book accommodation at the local hotel. Perhaps he would graciously escort her to the best guest bedroom. Robert could be so gracious. As Louise's oldest friend, she would surely be invited to stand by his side at the church tomorrow, and by the open grave. He would surely reach for her hand, and press it warmly, remembering their lovely shared holidays amid the romantic beauty of Caragh Lake. The poignant moment, never far from her heart, returned in full summer colours—the still lake with the tall trees reflected...that never-forgotten moment when Robert had pressed her very closely to him so that they were one with the reflections into the depths of the lake. He had murmured, "What a pretty little woman you are!"

In a dream of unfulfilled, but always hopeful, desire, Cassy wrote out a cheque for the bulky packages. The unexpectedly large amount of the cheque seemed fairly in keeping with the large expectations of the night.

When Cassy re-entered the kitchen, discreetly by the back door as instructed, Mrs MacNeill was taking a load of glassware from the dishwasher.

"Put the parcels over there," was her greeting, "and polish these glasses. Stack them on this tray and this one. They will be for after the funeral. Are you going to it? Well, okay. But you would be more useful here. I guess I will have to somehow manage on my own. Do you live near here? Oh, you did say you came a long way. Where are you staying? You don't have a place? There's a guest-room ready for Robert's sister. She can't make it for the funeral—she must be old, I guess, probably ancient if she was the eldest! You can stay in that room, if you want? Yeah well, you can bring in your bag later. Right now, there is a lot to do. And tomorrow will be worse! There will be a hundred, so Robert says, for drinks and sandwiches after the service—you got the ham? Great! Did you think of the whiskey? Okay okay. Those salad sandwiches would be better made in the morning, but there won't be time—that service is at ten. So let's get cracking."

Cassy gave up making attempts to interrupt. She felt it would be salutary to inform this woman of her own very special niche in this family-household. It seemed as if Cassy's diffidence towards Louise had transferred to this woman. There had not been a single mention of Louise, yet the woman was quite at home in Louise's kitchen. She had not, suddenly, been hired by the hour—that was obvious enough.

Puzzled, Cassy felt that by some underhand trick she herself had been co-opted onto the invisible staff. No thanks were due either for her help, or her cheque-book. Still, Cassy was smugly confident that when Robert was free at last of the calling mourners, he would correct Mrs MacNeill's erroneous impression. She pictured the change in the woman's rather arrogant face. Cassy, who loved clichés, thought the boot would be on the other foot then.

Robert did not appear. An uncertain timid pride prevented Cassy from asking questions. Mrs MacNeill's talk was totally concerned with the preparation of food. She was brisk and impersonal. Cassy stole a look at her as she flew about the big kitchen. She was certainly heading up to forty and her hair must surely be touched up? There was a lot of it all coiled around her head. Cassy thought she might be described as handsome rather than pretty. Maybe she looked American, like her voice, but Cassy had not met any Americans.

It was long after midnight when Cassy was told to fetch her overnight-case from her car. Mrs MacNeill led the way upstairs to a spacious corridor, hung with paintings and furnished with bookcases. Cassy was impressed with the opulence of it. Gazing around her, she forgot to speak.

"I am down at this end," said Mrs MacNeill, her voice somewhat lower than it had been in the kitchen, "This is the main bedroom on the right, and these two are empty. This last one on the left was got ready for Robert's sister, the door beyond it is the bathroom for it. Okay? I guess you will find anything you need, eh? Why don't I give you an early call? A touch of the vacuum here and there wouldn't come amiss!" Mrs MacNeill laughed softly as if to minimise the prospect of future toil. "Have a good night!" and the woman shut the door in a dismissive way without waiting for a like wish in return.

Cassy sat on the bed, her mind in a stunned silence. Then, disconnectedly, thoughts and emotions began to surface. Robert had never reappeared, in fact he was scarcely mentioned. And Louise, the poor dead wife who would be buried in the morning? Where was she? In a church? In a funeral parlour? Here, in the house? Was it possible that at this very moment Robert was keeping his lonely vigil by his dead wife, his handsome head bowed above her marble features?

It occurred to Cassy that no one had sympathised with her personally on the death of her friend, her lifelong friend, Louise. And not even a cup of tea since she arrived! And no mention of the cheque in payment for the drink and the meat!

Maybe Sadie was right? Sadie had often told her that she was like putty in people's hands. No, Sadie was wrong. You had to weigh in and do your part when there was a death in the house. Whether that MacNeill woman was here or not, Cassy felt she would have had to spend the night making sandwiches and running errands, and even vacuuming in the morning. It was all for Robert, really. To ease the pain of these days for him, and to get him over the sad ordeal of his wife's funeral, and to release him into a happier land, where he could look around in tranquillity, and recollect sunlit Caragh Lake and the faithful friend who had come there every summer for twenty years. They would go back in a little while to Caragh Lake, the unfulfilled caresses under the trees would blossom into...Cassy remembered the haunting music of an old romantic movie...would blossom into one night of love.

One night of love, she hummed the refrain as she prepared for bed. She was restored to serenity, living again in the cherished landscape of memory where there had always moved two figures only, set against the great lake and the ancient trees.

There was no heat in the water, no heat in the room, and flannel pyjamas would have been the right choice for the icy bed. In her filmy, flimsy, lacy nightie, Cassy had a hard task to keep in mind the promise of a morrow filled with appreciative love. Sleep was impossible. There was a dim bedside light but not a book in sight with which to pass the hours. All the luxuries of home were missing. She enumerated them, promising herself that she would bring all those luxuries into Robert's life: central heating, electric blankets, bedside phone and radio, perhaps a portable television in the kitchen. She missed the dogs. They slept in a basket in her room at home. She missed their dreamy snuffling, so contented and peaceful a sound. She began to worry about having put them in kennels, maybe they would catch colds. She should have asked Sadie to take them. Why did she not? She smiled to herself. It was because she had envisioned a longer stay than just for the funeral. She reassured herself it would be so. Just let tomorrow come!

For the fiftieth time she looked at her watch, it was five-thirty. A cup of tea, she thought, I will creep downstairs and make a cup of tea.

In the kitchen there was some heat from the banked-down Aga. She made tea and toasted some of the sandwiches she had made. She thought of what Sadie was always saying about her, "Never knows her own mind, up and down like a bloomin' yo-yo." And she smiled. It was true. A little thing made her happy and it did not take much to cast her down. The cup of tea had made a difference. The suppressed misgivings about Robert gave way to elation. This morning, all would be as her imagination pictured it should be. She would stand with quiet dignity beside a handsome Robert, being introduced to his illustrious friends, offering sherry to their charming sympathetic wives.

From the kitchen window she could see slivers of early light colouring the hedges. Perhaps the sun would shine all day. Now she would creep back upstairs very, very carefully and quietly. She would dress with the utmost attention to detail. Today she would look her very, very best. With an upsurge of resolution, she determined to refuse to vacuum.

On the turn of the staircase she paused.

The soft sound of the American woman's throaty laugh came from the dim corridor above. Cassy moved up another step, peering through the carved pillars of the bannister.

Robert and Mrs MacNeill were standing in each other's arms at the door of Robert's bedroom. The woman's hair was trailing down, thickly luxuriant. Robert was whispering, urgently, excitedly.

The woman's laugh was assenting and denying. Cassy caught the words "Old boaster!..." the rest of it was lost in Robert's embrace.

He took the woman to her room, kissing and caressing her with passion. Their nakedness seemed natural in the silvery colours of the dawn light, reminding Cassy of a painting she had seen in the National Gallery.

At last they parted, tenderly, lingeringly.

The shutters closed down on Cassy's imagination. An instinct of self-saving pride got her and her belongings out of the guest-room and into her car. To put distance between herself and Garlow Lodge was the only thought.

The miles rolling away behind her, Cassy came slowly to the realisation that the real distance was between the Cassy who had hurried joyfully to the funeral of a friend and the older, sadder Cassy who had attended the funeral of her own cherished dreams.

She knew, even now, there would be many future sleepless nights of frozen horror. She would see the dead Louise, her once-beautiful features grotesquely twisted, menace in her cold dead eyes as she watched the traitorous lovers in her marriage-bed. Cassy knew now that of course Louise was lying, stiff in her coffin, in the room beneath Robert's bedroom.

Cassy would know, too, in those future nights that while her experience had cleft a painful division into her character, frustrated longing would lead her endlessly back to Caragh Lake's deep reflections of undead desire.

There was consolation, nevertheless, in being Sadie's sister...Sadie who worried, Sadie who felt responsible. Sadie would take care of the turmoil inside. Sadie would not recognise it as such, because Cassy would tell the story differently. But tell it she would—every last detail of the whole sordid affair. Viewed coolly, of course, and very impersonally.

Cassy would soon be home. She could almost hear Sadie's voice. Sadie would go on and on, for hours at a time, castigating Robert. Sadie's phrases were predictable, almost enjoyable. Robert would be a filthy bastard, Mrs MacNeill would be a lascivious hussy, a whore or worse (an American, wouldn't you know, probably twice divorced), and poor dead Louise—a good faithful wife to that immoral lecher (my God, Cassy, you had a lucky escape!), poor Louise, not yet decently buried in her grave...the dirty swine ...the debauched libertine...There would be relief in listening to Sadie reviling Robert; there would be comfort. A kind of comfort, anyway.

The Love-Gift

Since the moment his wife returned from the town, Ned Murnane knew she was going to say something to him. She had that extra slow way of going about the kitchen, extra gentleness in the way she set out the ware for their meal. She had brought home the local newspaper. He sat by the fire, turning the pages, scanning for a familiar name of neighbour or townland.

"There's damn the divil a bit of news in the *Chronicle*," he growled, "not even the death of someone we know, " adding hastily, "Thanks be to God!"

She smiled at him. There was a quiet sweetness in the smile, almost an assurance, a confidence. There's something on her mind all right, mused Ned. She's going to broach something. She's giving me the eye like when we were courting. There's always a time for caution, he warned himself, when a woman gives you the eye.

"Who did you meet in the town?" Ned asked.

She set the tea-pot on the table, adjusting the knitted cosy around it. She smiled again, but Ned could see that this was a smile of ingratiation. She was aiming to give confidence to herself this time.

He knew he was right. He was a good judge. She

was not given overly to those smiles. Not indeed, Ned hastened to assure himself, that she was a soured woman. She was not. Nor a mean-spirited woman. Nevertheless, the loving smiles were reserved for the daughters and the grandchildren on a Sunday. That was natural, Ned felt. That was the way it ought to be. When a couple got to their age, giving the eye was a thing of the past.

"Did you not meet anyone, so?" he repeated.

"Beyond that I saw some of the women from around here when I was gathering the few things in the supermarket."

"And were you talking to no one then? You were gone long enough to be gossiping."

She bowed her head, and he was a small bit sorry. She was never a one for gossip. All the same, to be gone the whole morning and to come back silent as the grave was trying to a man's patience.

"It's the bicycle, Ned," she said softly. "I do have to walk the hills now."

This annoyed him.

"You had no call to go on the bicycle," he shouted. "If you had waited until Saturday I would have driven the tractor to the edge of town. Your own idea to go today. You never go on a Thursday—some fegary you took!"

Was it a tear he saw glistening in her eye? Suddenly an idea came out of nowhere. Was it to the doctor in the town she was going? He had not heard her complaining but with this woman you never could tell. She lived her life secretly and, Ned supposed, that was a proper way for women to live their lives. Those blathering women, like Tom Sullivan's wife, would put years on a man. Let women keep themselves to themselves—a man gets to know everything time enough.

"All right, all right then," he muttered, "you went to town, you talked to nobody, and you saw nothing!"

"Oh but I did!" she put in quickly, "I did. I saw something. I saw something in Mulrane's shop!"

Now Ned was puzzled. His instinct was right in the beginning. She had something to say. But Mulrane's shop?

"What would you see in Mulrane's shop? Sure women in their right mind wouldn't be going in there. Old Mulrane is as mad as a coot and his father before him ended up in the County Home. Sure they are the next best thing to tinkers, them and their old junk shop! Did anyone see you going in there?"

"I don't know if they did," she answered, visibly nerving herself to make a steady reply, "I wasn't noticing if anyone saw me. I only was looking at the…the thing…the…it in the window and I…"

"What did you see in the window?" roared Ned, "Speak up, woman! What did you see in the window of Mulrane's shop?"

The woman's face flushed with embarrassment and effort.

"I saw the present you said you would give me, Ned." Now Ned looked at her in speechless mystification. A present! What present?

"I never said I would give you a present. Are you feeling all right?"

Ned gave her his full attention. He examined her face closely. Her white hair, her white apron, her sensible shoes. She didn't look like a woman whose brain was a bit touched. Then you never could tell with this woman, so he changed his tone of voice to a kinder, less sarcastic note, "Are you feeling all right?"

"Yes. Yes I am. Thank you, kindly," she replied. There was a little pause. She took a deep breath, "You remember when I told you that this week we will be forty years wedded together? You said, 'Oh begor,' you said, 'we'll have to celebrate that. Forty years is it?' you said."

And Ned remembered. He remembered thinking that forty years was gone like a shout on the wind. And he remembered dismissing the thought of it from his mind. She was looking at him now, hopefully, affectionately.

"I asked you maybe if I could have a present from you for the memory of the forty years. Don't you remember?"

"And what did I say?" asked Ned.

"You said, 'Pick out something,' you said, 'and let me know.'"

So you picked out something in Mulrane's shop, thought Ned, and now you are letting me know. Oh, a man's instinct is a great thing. It lets a man beware when his pocket is going to be picked. Sharpen the wits now and have ready a good excuse why money is scarce.

"What's this going to cost me?" asked Ned in the manner of a man accustomed to dealing in thousands.

"'Tis this way, Ned," pleaded his wife, "it is not a very great sum of money. It is more like…would you give it for what it is?"

"What is it, woman?" demanded Ned in a voice one note lower than thunder. He prided himself on

126

being a patient man but not in the face of provocation, not with people who hedge around mincing words, "Out with it, can't you!"

He paid no heed that her lips were trembling.

"It's a...a...Chinese chair, Ned."

His face, and his mind, went blank. He was affronted. He could not take in her words. Something about the humble woman in front of him robbed him of his proper dignity. He felt on the knob of his chair for his cap. "I'm goin' up the yard," he muttered as he shut the door.

His field to the west was full of the evening sun. The four cows sauntered towards him. They were wintering out and soon they would be ready for the mart. He walked around them, admiring them, assessing their heavy flanks. His mind jumped away from the money they would fetch—in this world you could never call your money your own. Other people could spend it for you on unmentionable objects.

In spite of himself his memory recalled the proposed purchase of a commode. That would be about thirty-five years ago. It was not an object he fancied at the time. It was that sort of thing the gentry would go in for. Well, he had got out of that purchase by waiting until the subject ran out of steam. Then, four years ago the townland went on the public water scheme which proved him justified over barring the commode. A man does well to have built-in safeguards in this world. A deaf ear was one, poor eyesight, a bad memory. Everyone has tricks and you better be up to them.

He stood at ease for a long time up on the top ditch. Darkness was settling on his land when he plodded his way home. Framed in the kitchen window he saw his wife sitting waiting for him. The lamplight lent a sparkle to her white hair. There was a jar of snowdrops on the window-seat, completing the still picture. She sat like that every evening, tidy and silent, patiently waiting for his return before she would switch on the television. She loved the company of the television, but she would always wait. When he opened the back door, he barked out in an offhand way, "You can have that yoke you were talking about. How much is it anyway?"

Her face was radiant.

"It is five pounds, Ned, and if we take it, Mister Mulrane will give us the little table that goes with it for one pound more and he said he will deliver out to us for fifty pence only." Six pounds and fifty pence for Mulrane's old rubbish! Ned swore inwardly.

"I'll give you the money Saturday." He settled himself into his chair, "What's on the ould box tonight?" This enquiry informed her that conversation-time was over.

They never spoke in the bedroom any more than they would talk at a funeral. Ned was usually asleep before the woman had finished her night prayers. Tonight was different. Over the fingers linked into the rosary-beads, she was beaming up at him.

"Ned," she began shakily, "thank you for the...it was a..."

Ned knew she had no practice with the words unless she knew them by heart like her prayers, yet she was set on saying what was in her mind and a gentle determination carried her forward. "It was in a story we read in school. It was a story from The Golden Age. He was the King, I think. And he was giving the lady a present for every year. The present was called a love-gift. I have never forgotten that, a love-gift. And then I seen the...the...in Mulrane's shop, it was it...it was the...the..." The last words were muffled as the woman pressed her face into the white quilt.

"Humph!" muttered Ned, drawing the blankets around his ears. On Friday, Ned observed his wife was busy freshening up the small porch that formed the entrance to their house. It had never housed anything more than a few geraniums. Now he guessed the porch was to be the last resting-place for Mulrane's six pounds and fifty pence worth of rubbish. Well, he reasoned with himself, what she was up to now was not as bad as a full commode in a bedroom. Up the yard was the proper place and he had no doubt but that Mulrane's rubbish would find a home in the yard eventually.

The little porch was ready and shining on Saturday when Mulrane came with his van of bits and scraps.

"These are genuine antiques?" presumed Ned as he counted out six pounds and fifty pence for the two articles of black lacquer and red inlay.

Mulrane gave him his ferrety grin. "They are genuine Chinese. It would cost you more than that to go there and buy them!"

"Which I suppose you did," said Ned with a ton weight of sarcasm. In the kitchen, the woman dusted the two pieces carefully. Then with immense tenderness she polished them until they shone.

"Aren't they only beautiful," she breathed over and over. Ned did not agree. He averred he was not gone on black lacquer. There was a row of tiny red dragons carved across the rounded back of the chair.

"Those lads would stick into you if you were to sit on it," Ned pointed out. "But of course it's all only ornamental—who in their right senses would sit on the thing?"

"I would," his wife said softly. "Oh look, Ned, there's a little drawer in the table."

"Any money in it?" asked Ned facetiously.

"There's a weenshie key. Look, it fits the little drawer." She turned the key, the lock clicked smartly, the drawer was firmly closed. With infinite pleasure she placed and replaced the two pieces in the porch. At last she seemed satisfied to stand and gaze in admiration.

"Who will see them anyway?" Ned scoffed at her when he came in from the fields. "Anyone coming in here comes in by the kitchen. That old stuff is only ornamental. You'll never get the use out of them."

He knew the woman was unmoved by his jibes. Her quiet demeanour told of her contentment. She had had a dream, and her dream had come to pass. Someone, his father maybe, had told Ned that women are kittle cattle. Ned was sure that was true.

After mass on Sunday, the Blather Sullivans came up the lane to Murnane's. They were never invited: they always found a pretext. The usual one was an urgent loan, occasionally to be first with fresh news of a happening in the townland. This time, Ned surmised they had seen Mulrane's van passing up the lane on Saturday and he doubted they had slept a wink with the curiosity.

A spirit of boastful mischief got into Ned. He led the Sullivans around to the front porch. Throwing open the heavy door with a lordly gesture, he thus invited them to step inside.

"You've come to see our valuable antiques, have you? Look there! All the way from China! Oh, yes, didn't you know—herself is a great fancier of Chinese gewgaws! Oh didn't ye know? Cost me a bloody fortune! But you have got to pay for the genuine articles! If you want the best, I always say—provided you recognise it—well, you have to dig down deep..." He was slyly glancing from Tom Sullivan's big red gob to Missus Blather Sullivan's bulging cheeks when, out of the corner of his eye, he saw his wife standing at the kitchen door. She was looking and listening. All the bright serenity of her face was gone, covered over in a grey mist of age. It beats all, thought Ned, bolstering himself with vexation at her. Instead of crying with mirth at the way the Sullivans were lapping it up, this one was probably crying with a broken heart because I was jeering her old Chinese rubbish. I was the one that let her have it, wasn't I? Women, he had read it somewhere, had no sense of humour. He got rid of the Sullivans, walking them up the lane, covering their blather with blather of his own. At the first stile, he crossed over into his own fields putting distance between himself and the still-blabbing Sullivans. Out of sight, out of mind and face it later was sound policy. Not that he would ever consider himself in the wrong. It was the foolish way of women. It made a man wary.

Ned went home when, from afar, he saw the vehicles turning into the lane, betokening the Sunday visit of the daughters and their husbands and the grandchildren. Safety in numbers was another good trick when situations were a little delicate. Not that his wife would be likely to say something untoward to him but a fancied hurt would send her into herself like an old snail. Those fancied gripes were always too long-lasting for comfort.

Late in the evening, when the house was restored to quiet, and the woman gone to prepare for bed, Ned made his customary way into the porch to lock up for the night. He was half-expecting to find that the Chinese furniture had been banished up the yard, her grounds for acrimony hidden from sight. There was no change in the little room. His loud words of the morning had not left an echo to spoil the fragile peace. The red dragons were still puffing their way across the back of the chair. A small vase of budding twigs had been set on the Chinese table.

Ned tried the front door which he had so grandly flung open to the Sullivans. It did not budge. The big key was missing from its lifelong place. He looked around. The drawer of the table was shut, the woman's weenshie key removed for safe keeping. He juggled the Chinese table gently, he could hear the heavy porch-key sliding in the drawer. He slackened his jaws into a knowing grin.

A Late Flowering

The way legends grow in small towns, the people said you could set your watch by the Driscoll Brothers, Auctioneers and Valuers, Solicitors and Accountants. James, the senior partner, opened up on the dot of nine-thirty. Paul's big car, bigger every year, rolled up within the quarter-hour. He had stopped at the station to pick up his *Irish Times*. At ten, Young Tim arrived. He had probably given his dogs a run. The town called him Young Tim, because they remembered his father and his grandfather, for whom he was named. In fact, as everyone knew, he would never see forty again. The name persisted anyway, he was unaged in face and figure, a mild, cheerful and popular man. When Tim came through the glass doors of Driscoll Brothers at ten o'clock, the long street of the little town felt free to wake up and begin earning a living, mainly off the industry created by the Driscoll Brothers' widespread activities.

"Oh there you are," said James, "There is someone wants to see a piece of property out in the Demesne."

"The Demesne?" said Paul and Tim together, incredulity pitching their voices higher, and Paul added, "There is nothing in the Demesne that I ever heard of."

James had the Property For Sale ledger open. "Apparently it has been on our books for years. His lordship gave us the sale on one of his occasions of being hard up. It never sold. An old building. He has some woman interested in it."

Paul gave one of his famous handsome throaty laughs, "He must be hard up again. They say that her ladyship is taking him through the Divorce Court for everything he has got."

"That won't be a lot," was James's opinion. "Everything is entailed on the male side. The son in Australia will inherit when the lord finally snuffs it."

Tim had been looking for a map of the area. "There is a building marked," he said, "down by the river road. It is not a house, though. What does that double-round sign mean?"

James looked at the map. "That's the sign for a barracks. Their lordships of those days probably kept a troop of soldiers for protection against the unruly Irishry."

"Let me have a look at the map," said Paul as he took up his magnifying glass. Paul was the brother whose intellect and good looks had been his mother's pride. Tim often supposed in his own quiet way that every family must have one super ego, and he was content enough it should be Paul among the Driscolls.

"That is the old Constabulary barracks," Paul said. "We used to pass near there as kids, when Grandfather took us fishing."

"I never saw it," said Tim.

"Probably covered with trees," James thought, "It

looks like half a mile from the river, according to this map. What a pity I won't get to see such an interesting old relic. It can't have been lived in for sixty years. Will you take the woman out to see it, Tim? I am due in court in the afternoon."

"Due in court or paying court?" queried Paul softly.

"There must be several better places on the books than that," Tim said mildly, "We couldn't sell a dump in the woods. Waste of time going out there."

"Now, Young Tim, don't buck a challenge. You are at your best with elderly ladies," and Paul settled down to study his *Irish Times*.

James liked doing business with his lordship. He considered the old lord to be an eccentric in the grand manner, an almost extinct species. "His lordship must think he has an easy touch. He's sending the woman over at twelve-thirty. Let her make an offer, and I'll take it up to the Castle. He says we have the deeds, so maybe you would find them in his file, Tim?"

The lady client was easy to look at, and obviously very well-heeled. James usually took care of rich, female clients. Family rumour said he was on the look-out for a wife with money, age no object up to a certain limit. Certainly James would never have taken a good prospect out to look at this deplorable structure. Tim turned to look at the lady who was gazing up at the ruinous old house. He wondered why she did not walk away instantly. She reminded him of some famous film star of the old days: plenty of make-up, nice spiky eyelashes, smooth burnished cheeks, and a perfume that he supposed must be the exact perfume for the older woman. He felt full of apologies.

"I do assure you," Tim said, "that I have never seen this old house before. Although I am told that, as small boys, we often rambled through the Somerton demesne." And, he added to himself, that was forty years ago.

"Were you looking for birds' nests?" She had a dimpled smile and a pleasant voice. "I like the seclusion of it. I can hear birds singing in this silence."

"Whatever about that," Tim said, "this house was never built for family living. The way that long hall sticks out, way off centre. And those uneven windows, no symmetry."

Tim was not given to running down property, but even James would agree that the commission on this ruin was not worth the usual sales-talk. He looked at the specifications again: spring-well, quarry-stone walls treble width, gun emplacements. Gun emplacements? Now he noticed the narrow slits on each side of the windows, and he wondered aloud: "Lord Somerton's constabulary have been gone a long time...he must be hard up indeed if he thinks to sell this..."

She was smiling again. "I hardly think he is hard up but divorces do cost a lot. This protruding hall? Yes, Athelstan did tell me this place was built as a constabulary barracks about two hundred years ago."

Athelstan! Tim supposed he had heard Lord Somerton's name, but he had never heard it used. Athelstan! The familiar way she said it! In this county, Castle Somerton is a tourist attraction. Its owner is known to the town as "his lordship," no capital letters and a deal of sarcasm.

They opened the heavy door and stepped into the long hall. This ran the length of the house with a glass-paned double-door at the back. Briars grew over the glass. Tim could easily picture queues of ragged peasants, standing in mute misery while the Lord Somerton's constabulary stamped their travel warrants for Van Diemen's Land. The lady, on the contrary, appeared entranced with this hall. "What a marvellous picture-gallery," she murmured, "only needing the correct lighting."

She opened a door off the hall. It led to a big room with windows to front and back. The rounded windows would give a view of the woods if the trailing ivy were removed.

"Mr Driscoll, take a look at this fireplace! And the half-panelled walls! Quite dry!"

Dry rot, Tim thought, and he reflected on the swarming millions of wood-beetles behind the wooden panels. Two hundred years of them.

She was examining the fireplace, with its surround of black pilasters. "This could never be marble, could it? So black, and feel the coldness of it," she invited, "as cold as if it came from Italy only yesterday."

"There is black marble in Kilkenny," Tim said, a little defensively.

"Kilkenny!" she echoed softly, "How about that!"

She paced the room from side to side. "I am placing my chairs and a big couch. I am thinking of party nights."

Tim gazed up at the curved ceiling. Parties and picture-galleries in the middle of these woods?

There were two other rooms on the other side of the dreary hall. One, she decided, was the shape for a library because it had well-placed windows, and although it had a very ordinary fireplace, at least it was there, "Ready," she said, "to be ingle-nooked."

She was pretty and very pleasing but Tim wondered if perhaps she was a bit light in the head. Ingle-nooks went out with storm-lamps.

The other room, another view of the woods, would be a guest-room, "taking its water from above for the *en suite*."

"But wouldn't you have to have a kitchen?" Tim asked, puzzled. "Isn't this the normal place for a kitchen?"

She took his hand in a very friendly way. "Let us see if we could have an upstairs kitchen, even a galley, with plenty of room for a dining/living room. If all the main plumbing is upstairs, it will be easier to have the guest-room *en suite*, and also a downstairs cloak and wash-up."

The stairs were of stone, curved on the inside wall of the house and lit by the uneven windows which Tim had criticised earlier. Within, they were acceptable enough, having deep embrasures. "These windows are ideal for colourful potted plants," the lady observed, "I love late-flowering plants. They come into their own when summer is fading. I love them, don't you?"

Luckily enough, the rooms seemed to correspond to her quick planning. "But, of course," she smiled, "I should need to take accurate measurements, and draw a proper lay-out." Tim did not dare to look at her for fear her eyes would have become strange. A lay-out for this antiquated heap! She was a bit dippy. Pity. He thought it only honest (and fearing again that she could not be seeing correctly) to draw her attention to the gaping hole in the roof, the stripped laths, the crumbling plaster. The dimples of her smile deepened. "Athelstan warned me of all this. He also warned me not to get ripped off by the local contractors! Mr Driscoll, let us walk now in what will be my garden—if I buy. Athelstan has promised shrubs and roots and all sorts of plants."

Athelstan again! But maybe she had a husband? Here I am, thought Tim, hitting fifty and I have never learned to sum up a woman. Paul, to use his own words, would have her taped and be on his way home to dinner long since. If I have learned anything from my brothers in this house-selling business, it is to beware of whimsical women. Women get whims about houses, *especially* about houses, and a week later the husband phones in to say the wife has changed her mind: "Just a vague idea she had!" Never having been married, Tim was never sure if it was the not-so-vague husband who had changed her mind for her. Nowadays, best not to say so. Three bachelors, and the bossy married sisters were quick to check their sexist opinions if they dared voice them. However, right now, better find out if the husband has a voice?

"Despite the isolation," Tim said, "this place is not too remote from the golf club. That is, if you play? Or perhaps your husband plays?"

By her smile, she recognised his ploy for information. Her reply was courteous. "That I should be so lucky as to have a golf-playing husband! Nor do I play." Now she turned and faced him, "The decision will be all mine, when I make it, Mr Driscoll."

For some obscure reason, he hesitated to ask her to call him Tim; the glory of Athelstan was overripe for the commonplace Tim. They drove back to town. She got into her car outside the Driscoll brothers office, and prettily bade him good evening.

Paul wanted a full report at dinner that evening. He had glimpsed the client as she drove off in her car. An American heiress, no less. From New York—where else! He had heard she was loaded! Since no one could have told him this, it was the usual Paul bluff. "Good-looking, isn't she?" he asked.

"You could say that," Tim answered, "But she is not young."

"It's a loaded *young* one he wants," put in James, "A loaded slightly older one would do me. What's her name again?"

"Mrs Fantoy," Tim said shortly, and then he could not resist adding, "She calls Lord Somerton Athelstan!" He should have enjoyed their reaction to this. They ho-ho-ed and ho-hummed for nearly five minutes until the name Athelstan lost its hilarity for Tim, and became strangely repugnant. The whole town had followed his lordship's divorce with intense interest. Could Mrs Fantoy have been the reason? What kind of a name was that? Fantoy? Paul, the family encyclopaedia, had never heard of that name. A made-up name, do you think? Could Mrs...er...er...Fantoy be the new mysterious love? "The Femme Fatale of the Costly Divorce?" asked Paul, in capitals.

"Lord Somerton must be in his late seventies," Tim countered their raucous innuendoes, "He's over the hill!"

"There is no such thing as 'over the hill,'" James declared, "until a man has been pronounced in rigor mortis."

"In rigor mortis for a fortnight," added Paul. According to the married sisters, Paul had a terrible reputation with women. He took that to mean he was devastatingly attractive.

"Is Mrs Fantoy installed in Castle Somerton?" enquired James.

"With Athelstan?" enquired Paul.

Tim always took the spaniels for a walk after dinner. That night, he walked them twice as far as usual but he was not tired enough to sleep. He kept asking himself: If what Paul and James suspected was true, why would Mrs Fantoy want to buy a derelict dump in the woods, and presumably spend thousands to make it fit to live in, when it belonged to her lover anyway (if Somerton was her lover), when her next move would be into Castle Somerton, and in due course, she would become the Lady Somerton. She did not look in the least like the divorced Lady Somerton who was very tall and dangerously slender...it was said she lived on a lettuce leaf and twenty cigarettes an hour. This is ridiculous, Tim thought restlessly, but why would Mrs Fantoy live in a moth-eaten ugly barracks if she has a castle in her sights. Why? Why?

Tim put the puzzle to James and Paul over breakfast. James saw no difficulty. "When money's no object, those sort do those sort of things."

"Maybe the pair of them are making an Agapemone!" smiled Paul, who read peculiar stuff, and came out with odd things at times.

"Whatever the hell an Agapemone is!" Tim shouted, and surprised himself by banging the door loudly.

Mrs Fantoy phoned the office. Would Mr Driscoll take her out to the house again? Tim asked if he could take her out to lunch? "When we have a deal," she said, "perhaps you would ask me again?" It was a long time since Tim had asked a lady out to lunch. There had been many girls through the years but no regrets when they married other men.

This time Mrs Fantoy had a note-pad, and a business-like tape measure. She was quite expert in her careful measurements. Tim became very uneasy as he watched her earnest face pondering over the notes she made.

"May I ask you something, Mrs Fantoy?"

She looked up, "Of course."

"Do you want this place?" he asked. "I mean to say, it is a real shack. It will cost so much to do up, and after all that, it will still be miles from any sort of amenity. Very lonely. Think of the winter months. That is, if you will really be on your own?"

"You surely are concerned for me, aren't you. It is a grand feeling to have someone concerned for me. Thank you, Mr Driscoll. Yes, I shall be on my own. Mr Driscoll, people in New York would kill for a place like this!" and she was smiling again.

The surge of triumph, to hear Paul and James were probably wrong, was totally irrational.

"I have decided to buy," Mrs Fantoy told him. "I shall tell Athelstan today. Mr Driscoll, I will be depending on your advice with regard to the local contractors of building, and plumbing especially. You will help me?"

Why him? Why not Athelstan? But Tim knew the answer to that one. The locals would screw Lord Somerton. It was the traditional thing to do.

On the hand-over day, James and Paul were dressed like dandies to meet with Mrs Fantoy. The inner office was rank with the smell of after-shave. James was first off his mark. "May I have the pleasure of your company for dinner, Mrs Fantoy?"

"Thank you, I should like that," she said, and then she glanced up at Tim, "You came first, didn't you?" He could only nod, humbly grateful that she had remembered. Now James got that smile made of spiky eyelashes and an elusive dimple, "So tomorrow night, would that suit?"

"When will it be my turn?" asked Paul, with a very winning smile. When they were kids, Paul was the handsome brother, doted on by the sisters. Tim thought the adoration had gone to his head. The family said he had a woman in Dublin. Paul's big car hit the Dublin road most weekends, and he went off to Greece every year with someone, maybe the Dublin woman. Paul used to say: a man is time enough at forty-eight. He hadn't said that recently, but he fancied himself as much as ever. James, on the contrary, was plain. He was confident he knew the ropes where women were concerned. Some day soon, he would land the big fish. Meanwhile, a man must keep his hand in practice if only with the local beauties, married or single. A man's health depended on it.

It took fully six months for all the contracting work to be completed on the erstwhile constabulary barracks. In that six months, the three Driscoll brothers courted Georgette Fantoy ardently. Lunches, dinners, theatres, horse-shows, even art exhibitions. James, perhaps feeling his more-than-half-a-century, said, "You name it, we are doing it!

The local yokels graduating into the sophisticated suitors!" The bossy sisters laid odds on. Tim was quite sure that he was not the favourite in the race.

And all the time, Georgette continued to live in Castle Somerton. The brothers knew one another's strength, the unknown factor was the divine Athelstan.

"She is playing the lot of us, one against the other," complained Paul.

"It's an exhausting bloody business!" moaned James, "and the trouble is, she hasn't got an affectionate bone in her little body. No give!"

Tim was very glad to hear that Georgette had no give for the masterful James. Tim knew now that he had fallen in love (and what an inadequate phrase that was for him), fallen deeply and irrevocably in love. He knew it when Georgette sat into the car beside him after their very first inspection of the old place. Her perfume seemed to activate a sense of fragrance within him, almost as if ethereal shoots of tenderness had broken the hard desert of no-desire. Each morning he was closer to despair.

Daily, nightly, he assessed his chances and his brothers' chances. They were no longer young, but then neither was Georgette. They were free, but then was she? Was she? Paul had fortunes amassed in land and he was a very prepossessing man. To Tim, it was plain that Georgette was highly amused by Paul. James owned property right across the midlands, and women found him wonderful—he had had plenty of them after him, or so he said. Tim was very successful on the stock market, an inherited flair, but would a woman like Georgette find that an added attraction? Paul said constantly that women were spoiled for choice; a man had to have, Paul insisted, added attractions. All three brothers, of course, had the business, which was booming.

Yes, Tim reflected, they were wealthy men, but they would never rank with the Somertons, and their centuries of breeding, and in-breeding. Georgette referred, all the time, to Athelstan: warmly, familiarly, while eating the Driscoll dinners and taking the Driscoll expert advice.

Maybe she was simply playing games with the Driscoll brothers? Even a game, Tim thought, kept her in his view. This passion for Georgette was the only passion that had ever happened to him in all his near-fifty years. He knew she was one year older than he was, and somehow that pleased him. He knew a lot of things about her by the end of six months. Although she always reminded him of some long-ago film star, she had not been an actress, she was a successful architect. Her husband was killed in Vietnam. She had one son, aged thirty, and now married. She had made a solemn vow to herself that she would retire in good time to enjoy her old age in Ireland. Getting the old house was a first step in that direction. "Ireland," she said constantly, "was the ideal place to run down slowly." Some days, she said, "settle peacefully," other days, she said, "jog along joyfully." She was a happy woman.

Tim knew so much, and yet so little. What if Ireland should be a disappointment? And where did Athelstan come in? For whom had he put aside the wife of his lifetime? For whom was the expensive divorce worthwhile?

Georgette's furniture had come, and she had arranged it beautifully. Pictures were hanging in the long hall, now subtly lit. Already the garden was taking shape; meanwhile flowers from Castle Somerton filled the vases.

"I can see myself becoming very accustomed to that wonderful bed in Georgette's place," announced James at breakfast. "Making-the-mind-up time has come for me. I have a solitaire out on spec from my pet jeweller. Take heed, my brothers, tonight is the night I am going to pop the question."

Paul took this in good spirits, probably thinking that James hadn't a hope in hell, "I will give you first chance of refusal, old son! Age being honourable! Comes before beauty, they say! So I'll go next. From a certain hint she dropped on our last encounter, I would say my chance is *sine dubio*." Always the legal big-head.

Georgette had dropped no hint to Tim. She must surely give a sign if she was prepared for a proposal? It was just not in her nature to hurt. She would not lead a man on only to cast him down coldly. Had she led them on, or had they pursued madly? Tim wanted to rush out and shout his proposal from the roof-top. He could not. You were born into the Somertons, or you never got there. They married among themselves. No, he had to wait for a sign. Wait and ache.

James's face next morning was non-committal. "She parried me!" he said. "I would say she could be good for a re-run! Enjoyed it, don't you know! Got a kick out of my performance, I would say!"

Tim was not impressed, and Paul gave James a very superior grin.

Yesterday morning, the handsome Paul steamed

into the dining-room. Now *his* decision time had come. Georgette had consented to be picked up at six, and he had booked his candle-lit table-for-two in a famous, and expensive, Dublin hotel. No doubt he had equipped himself with the biggest diamond in the town jeweller's shop. On spec, Tim hoped, and not on the *sine dubio* hint she was supposed to have dropped.

Tim was not a drinking man, but on his way to view property at the far side of the county, he dropped into every pub along the road. He watched a junior hurling match in a country school. He played darts in a shebeen, down a road he was never on before.

Yesterday was the longest, loneliest day in Tim's life.

He must have arrived home some time because he was at the table this morning, waiting for Paul's triumphal entry.

"He never came home at all!" announced James dramatically. "His bed was not slept in!" Tim's heart, poor battered symbol, sank down to the depths. James was ho-ho-ing and hum-humming, until Tim felt like crashing a fire-iron on his head.

"Don't look for me in the office today!" Tim shouted, "I won't be there!"

He put the spaniels in the car, and he drove out to Georgette's lodge. He had to know if neither of them had come home. Or he had to see for himself if Paul were installed in the midst of Georgette's luxury, like a king enthroned. James was licked, he was out of the race.

Georgette was in the garden; she was sitting in the garden; she was simply sunning herself. Tim forced himself to the point of speech:

"Did you enjoy your dinner with Paul last night?"
She showed no surprise. "I did not go. I told him I
had such a dreadful headache. I told Paul it was
probably sunstroke…of course, it may not have been
sunstroke…"

So his brother Paul had gone to Dublin, where,
apparently, there was always a welcome. Good—
that reduced the odds.

"Georgette, may I ask you a question?"

"Anything, Tim."

"How much do you like Lord Somerton?"

"Oh very much! He is a sweetie, always so kind!
Not very nice of me to say this: but he gets very
boring. I am not really into the history of fire-arms! I
was so glad when my little lodge was ready and I
could move in."

"So, you are not going back to live in Castle
Somerton?"

"Tim, don't sound so cross. This is my home
now."

"That's all right, then. I am on my way to take the
spaniels down to the river."

And visit the jeweller in the town.

"May I take you out to dinner tomorrow night?"
Tim asked as if it were an afterthought, very cool
and casual. "That is, if your headache will be
better?"

Georgette was smiling like that long-ago film star,
whose face had lit his teenage years with the
expectation of beauty. "Tomorrow night, for sure,"
she said. Tim waited. Had he been given the come-
hither sign? At least, he was still in the race.

He was walking away across the river road, when

she called his name:

"Tim! Tim! Athelstan is my late husband's second cousin."

Ilex Lutea

M onday 2 August: I have been sitting by the window, thinking of your suggestion that I keep a diary until I go back. Come back in a month, you said. I suppose you were thinking that in a month from now I would have forgotten all the thoughts I should communicate to you, to help you to deal with me.

But, Doctor, I do not forget. When I go silent to your probing questions, it is not because I have forgotten the answers. Nor is it ever, as Sister Superior insists, because I am wilful. Sometimes your questions open up so many other more complex questions in my mind, that I am baffled by the enormity of my problem in your eyes. When I am alone, quite alone, all problems disappear.

I am alone now, sitting in this room familiar to me since earliest memory. This is my grandmother's chair. Long ago, she used hold me on her knee. My mother, too, liked this chair. Often I remember her sitting here in the evening light, waiting for my father's car to turn into the drive. After his death, she went on waiting here. She seemed content. Too late, I realised that she was merely waiting for her life to end. Soon she, too, was gone.

I have moved to the southern window. I must not

seem to be waiting for Sally when her car comes speeding to the front door. What did you think of Sally, Doctor, when she came to take me home yesterday? She made an impression on you straight away! I could see that. Don't you think she is lovely? I am so proud of her, my daughter and my friend. She is full of life, and full of resource. She looks like a model in a woman's magazine, yet she has acquired all those academic honours. She is compassionate and tolerant, never afraid to show affection. Last night, she tucked the bedclothes around me, kissing my hands and my cheeks, whispering silly endearments just like a little girl whose mummy had been away.

Tuesday: I woke up this morning thinking I must put something significant in my diary for you. But what is there significant in my coming home? My thoughts and my affections never left this house. Only my body was taken from it.

This was my bedroom when I was a girl. The early sun always glints from the window into the mirror. Sally thought it would be warmer here than in the big room next door. And it is. Sally does not know that in the year she was in Canada, it was less lonely to sleep alone in this single bed. Alone, I was less prone to tears. I was going to tell her about that when she came with a breakfast-tray. One glance at her face, beaming love and concern, and I knew I would not tell her today.

I have learned that if I try to tell anything of the conflict within, I may say too much. I must defend and justify. I think I should fill the unexplained gaps with lengthy explanations, which in themselves must be explained. Sister Superior, in denying the

156

need for any woman in the ward to take a secret pride in being special, impressed on me that a proud woman would hesitate to be a bore. So, no lengthy explanations. To be properly proud is certainly attractive. But does it bar communication? And, regrettably, I needed communication so badly. Did you know that, Doctor? Is that significant? You thought me singularly untalkative, you said.

I have brought the diary down to this window again. I meant to write more about myself, but instead I have been gazing out at the garden. The garden looks worn, in need of care. Perhaps tomorrow I could go out with a hoe, maybe tidy it a little.

Long ago we had a gardener. He was not a real qualified gardener, just a handyman called Old Jim. He came, with the house, from my grandmother. He was some great age even then, and when he died he was not replaced. My father loved the garden; very especially he loved roses. In summertime he never went on holiday for fear of missing the best of the roses. It is true that he talked to the roses, knowing each one by its given name, and complimenting or commiserating with each one in turn. They seemed to be all lady roses: Zepherine Drouhin, Ena Harkness, Helen Traubel, Dorothy Perkins, Emily Grey, and Cleopatra—a red and yellow beauty to whom he was devoted. I often heard Old Jim muttering curses, at the weeds among the vegetables and when he was cutting back the loganberries. I remember the taste of those loganberries, warm against the wall.

I took a long pause there. You told me so often that memory tends to be melancholy. I am sure you must know because you have studied the subject from all sides. The way my memory works is like a sunny lane into ancient happiness.

You questioned me a lot about my childhood. If I could root out the minute particle of malice to be found in my babyhood, or perhaps in my teens, if I could view it and rationalise it, then I would be able, you said, to lay hold of the stress in my adult life, and to deal with it. Simple, you implied, if I would only co-operate.

Forgive me, Doctor. My silence was plain bewilderment. My childhood was happy through and through. Your questions forced the question on me: was I spoiled by happiness? Your questions, albeit put kindly, were always seeking for some evil emanation of which I find no trace. I see only love.

One day you asked me, with apologetic diffidence, was I a little in love with my father? I shook my head. To be explicit does not always lay bare the truth. Had I said yes, you would have discovered something about me....something deeply rooted in me, which, when analysed, would identify a tendency in me. I did not believe you would be nearer the truth, and so I shook my head.

But I was in love with my father—passionately in love with him. I loved the look of his eyes on me, a deepening caress. I loved the fragrance of his breath when he kissed me. Rich cigar smoke, port wine, roses—all evoke him. Most of all, I loved the way he loved my mother, openly, ardently. He had invented so many phrases for her beauty, that sometimes she hid her blushes against his shoulder. Grandmother, with whom we lived, was in love with him, too. She worshipped him. Daily, she enquired about his sleep, his health, his appetite. Daily, she marvelled at the superb quality of him.

It is infinitely sad that you should believe all that ecstasy of love in my young life to be merely a foreboding of melancholy for my middle years.

Wednesday: I went into the garden. The arbour is gone. Torn down. Rooted up. I looked; I searched; it is not there; it is gone. I stood there crying. I wanted to cry and cry and cry so that my heart must break. Just in time, I remembered Sister Superior's voice grating on about any indulgence in tears. At my age I should have learned self-discipline, she said, the lack of it was half my trouble. So, trying even now for discipline, I had dried the tears before Sally came home. Tears would banish the lovely smile for which I wait each evening.

But the arbour...

Thursday: You see, I remember when the arbour was planted. I remember the care with which my father chose the exact spot for planting. "An arbour must give a vista of the garden in the evening sun; it is in the evening one rests in one's arbour," he smiled at us, "one must be warmed and sheltered as one rests." It was important to plant the exactly right cuttings in the exactly right arc. The arc would later take a curved high-backed bench. Later still, there was a garden-table.

The cuttings were the subject of a winter-long debate. Finally, the evergreen *Ilex Lutea* was chosen for its biddable meshing qualities. I was seven then. I recall my mother saying that the sound in *Ilex Lutea* conjured-up a vision of trees that swayed like singing mandolins. Trusting my father absolutely, I

159

did not express disappointment when the *Ilex Lutea* turned out to be little slips of ordinary green holly.

The arbour was slow in forming. My father snipped and shaped it constantly. By my fourteenth birthday, a few days before Christmas, it had grown vividly into a perfect cave. The spiky, glistening leaves were studded with red berries. The high-backed, curved bench had been made by our local carpenter; it was securely fitted against the intertwining branches. Overhead, there was scarcely a chink of sky.

All summer long, year after year, the arbour was another room, a garden-room. Sometimes, my father would place two or three roses in a vase on the table there. We sat in our half-circle, admiring them. My mother's work-box, Grandmother's spectacles, my book—all furnished the table in the arbour, making it special and cosy.

The arbour had brought so much pleasure into my life for so many years. How could someone tear it down? For I knew who had done this. I knew there was one who would tear down and root up.

I knew because I had been rooted-up out of this house, rooted up and thrown down, and locked away.

Friday: Last night when Sally came to tuck me into bed so lovingly, her tenderness melted the hard edge I had imposed on my tears. I asked, dolefully, about the destruction of the arbour. When?

"But, darling," she smiled, "don't look so sad. I think that old holly-arbour has been gone for years and years."

She is thinking of something else. There was an old wood-shed, it was in need of repair and it rotted away. I feel very firm and clear about the arbour. It was there, in all its glory of green and red, when he delivered me into the hands of Sister Superior. It was always green and red at Christmas, that is the season of *Ilex Lutea*. And in Sister's office, there were sprigs of holly on the holy pictures.

I do remember the beauty of the arbour because I went out there to sleep on the night of the beating. It was Christmas night.

Will it help you if I set this down, Doctor? Will you find it significant, I wonder. A struggle was forced on me to make me...conform. To make me stay in bed, in that other room, in this house. There was talk of snow and cold. There were blows and tears, someone fell on the stairs and there was no one to help. But that time, I won. I am quite clear; I remember getting to the arbour. It was all gold and full of rustling music...*ilex lutea...ilex lutea*. The arbour was there that night, my father's arbour. It has been destroyed because I loved it. At last, this telling tells you a fact.

His head was bandaged and he drove the car. I sat in the back with two nurses who gripped my arms. There were tall iron gates, a room with an electric fire. He signed papers. He pecked my cheek. He was gone.

Here is another fact: I never longed for his return. In all the grisly humiliation that has befallen me, in the nightmare of narrow grey beds, slop-pails, vacant formless faces, in the pathetic loneliness of knowing that I had been dumped and deserted, even in the intellectual loneliness of no books and no music, even then I have never wanted him back. There is no burden on me of regret or remorse, and no tender memory.

To look back to his coming into this house, after my mother's death, is to see a stranger. I remember better the face of the lawyer, with whom he came, whose junior he then was. After twenty-five years of sharing my life with him, he remained a stranger. When you asked me to analyse my feelings towards him, or when you tried to do so in face of my apathy, you were talking of someone I have never known. And now I never wish to know.

At some one moment my mind was cleansed of him.

Later on Friday: I hid the diary when Sally came in. She had bought a dress for me, and shoes—elegant shoes, and such a pretty dress. She knows I adore clothes, I always have. The dress is a perfect fit. I must find an occasion to wear it soon. Then Sally fixed my hair. She said so many funny and very uncomplimentary things about Sister Superior's idea of "off-the-ear" hairstyles that she reduced both of us to laughing.

When I was alone I was flooded by hopeless tears. A mental home is a desperate place, Doctor. Being feminine ceases to be a special feeling. Being scarcely human is a stage already reached by some. In a mental home, the stages downward come more easily than the struggle upward. But then, the struggle upward leads only back to cold reality.

Tonight, the glamorous idea of being a lovely woman again was made to appear worthwhile. Is it? What good has it done me before? And for whom should I look attractive?

I have not asked of his whereabouts, nor have I set my mind to the thought—until now.

When his image left my senses, there were

sometimes nights for sleeping. I no longer staggered around that cell, falling over the clown's gown into which Sister had me strapped each night.

...Your eagle eye will notice that I have torn three pages from the diary, three pages of fantasising. It will not help you to know what were my unsleeping dreams when they locked the cage. You already suspect that my problems with adult relationships are rooted in a child's passion for her father. Should I now reveal that my father did indeed come to comfort me in the narrow grey bed, you would at last be sure that you had the key to set me free. You would set me free to return to him, the hero-husband, wherever he is holding himself in readiness.

So gradually, I came to know that I had the lunatic's choice. I could continue wilful and endure the hateful home until death released me. Or, I could be cured and return to the life before the home, until death do us part. There were many women there (as you well know, Doctor) who were released "into custody," only to escape again "into detention." In a year or two, I would be back with you, permanently, all choice gone.

Much later: I think sleep is eluding me tonight. I will try to write a little more for you. If you look back on your notes, you will trace the upward slope of my improvement from the day I broke my silence to answer a question. It required some cunning to let days elapse between apathy and interest. Since I had refused "with convulsions of rage" (Sister Superior's words) to accept any visit from him, it was necessary to have you find out from him when Sally would return from Canada. I began, then, to concentrate on the passing of the weeks, showing a little advance, a little slackening, a further alertness.

When Sally came, it was urgent to find out into whose custody I was to be released. Had I asked the relevant question, I would have been locked up immediately. Lunatics do not get answers to questions, no matter how relevant. Lunatics get kindly kidding or impossible promises. When the time came, I had to take a chance, and go passively.

As it happened, Sally did not mention him. Each day, my hopes have multiplied. Five days I have been home, home in this beloved house which has been home ever since memory began—five days alone with Sally, sometimes totally alone. I have been happy and contented as I always was long before he came.

I was twenty then, when my mother died.

Saturday: I have been so lucky with the weather and this morning it is glorious. Sally is at home all day today. Just now she is cooking lunch, something very special, she says. I was sent out of the kitchen. I am to relax with a glass of sherry. We walked in the garden in the early sun. My eyes searched everywhere for the arbour, but we did not talk of it. I needed more to bask in her cheerfulness.

I have tried, doctor, to keep a sequence to my thoughts in writing this diary. I recollect only too well the questions you asked me continuously during all those months. Yet, even pondering them, I seem not to have progressed beyond the night it was decided to have me locked up.

Our doctor came. It was not his decision—he prescribed sedatives. It was my husband's decision. He suggested that I submit myself voluntarily. That I agreed to this self-immolation, that I applauded this suggestion with hysterical clapping, was a measure of my desire to be shut of the sight of him.

Between my childhood and that night, there seems to be a lifelong gap.

Life began to be insufferable when Sally went to Canada. With her departure, real life ended. The pretence, the effort, was no longer worthwhile. The wonder of her had blotted out the loneliness, negatived the incompatibility. You have seen her, Doctor. I saw you take a second glance, a longer look. She is so special.

Sally was our only child. For years I prayed for another child. For years I submitted myself to harsh, loveless couplings in the hope of a family. It was not to be. The coupling became wrong and sinful, a recreational sexuality that was distastefully practised on me. My compliance was taken for granted. I was reminded that our religion compels a wife's compliance to a husband's demand. Love, tender longing, played no part. Lust had to be obeyed at regular intervals. There is more, much more, but beware of self-pity. And already, that is more than I had intended to write. Does it answer all the patient hours of probing questions with which you tried to break my wilful silence. "If you could only face the simple truth of your worry," you said.

I had faced it, Doctor. Years ago. I had faced my revulsion. Facing it had not resolved the fact that it would go on, until death do us part.

Sally is calling me for lunch.

Very late on Saturday: During lunch, the phone rang. Sally often has phone-calls. This one took rather a long time. When she returned to the table, her sunny face was clouded. She placed her cutlery neatly on the plate, she seemed disinclined to eat any more.

"That was Dad," she said quietly.

I knew. A sort of panic had registered in my throat.

"He wants to come and see you tomorrow?"

I could feel the familiar storm rising inside me. Sally came around to my side of the table. She put her arms about me so lovingly, pressing her face against my hair. Some perfume she was wearing distilled its fragrance.

I knew he had not moved out. Through the glass door of the old cloak-room, I had seen his suitcases, his grey valise. They are stacked on the wooden rack, as they have been for twenty-five years. They have a light veil of dust. They are not going anywhere. They are here to stay.

I belong in this lovely house as nowhere else on earth; yet it is I who am forced to leave. Am I to be housed now and forever with you and Sister Superior? Am I to be forever dressed as she deems fit in padded gown with buckled straps? My hair chopped above my ears, my view of high stone walls topped off with jagged glass?

"Darling, you haven't answered me," Sally was saying softly, "Dad would like to come and see you tomorrow, what do you think?"

I tried to get a firm grip on the chaos beginning inside me. I tried to smile, sanely.

"When? What time?"

Sally hugged me closely. "Don't get upset, Mum, I will be here. Any time that suits you. Morning, afternoon, evening...I promised to ring him later today. The poor old chap is very distressed because I sent him off for a few days. I wanted you all to myself, darling. It's been gorgeous after all those months away. Don't cry, Mum, please don't cry. I will be here always...I promise you, always and always."

That shocked me into sense. Sally to be with me always. Oh no. I loved her far too much to trap her like that. I had a fleeting vision of Sally as a dried-up old spinster who had sacrificed her life, maybe her love, for her silly, foolish mother. The fact that I could not manage my life on my own was not a reason for wrecking her life also.

I knew such thoughts must not be revealed. I must not pretend even to suspect that she was making plans to bolster up my future. Nor must I let her think that her being with me makes it possible for me to soldier on.

At the instant she said the words, "I'll be here always," the inevitability of my course was set. Sense, reason, peace, came pouring into my mind. Please remember that, Doctor...sense, reason, peace.

"Yes, yes," I said, "the evening would be best. Perhaps about seven. I want to visit my parents' grave in the afternoon."

Sally looked wonderful. All the cloud had gone from her eyes. She was radiant with relief. "I'll drive you over to the cemetery, darling. It is such a lonely old place now that they have their new cemetery. We'll bring flowers from the garden."

"I think I would rather go on my own," I replied, "you never liked that cemetery, you used to say it was 'ghosty.' It is not a long walk. You have tea ready when I get back!"

I gave Sally my best and most loving smile, "tea and that cake you made."

Sunday morning: It was late when we went to bed. Sally talked about Canada, and a man there who is a very special friend. In her words, I detected shades of withdrawal from this friend and from her life in Canada. I longed to say: "Wait. You will be free." Lunatics must be wary. Their listeners are apt to be alerted. I was quiet without being totally silent.

Being quiet was not hard. I was at peace, all chaos stilled and tidied away. The decision of my last choice, an inevitable one, had been taken by forces within me, and beyond me, too strong to be resisted.

This morning, I am wearing the new clothes Sally gave me for my home-coming present. I have inspected myself in the long mirror, and I think I look well. My skin is clear and fresh. The flowers have been cut, they lie waiting in white paper. It is agreed that I shall go to the old cemetery after lunch.

The weather continues glorious. It will be peaceful beside my parents' grave today. Always in the old cemetery, there are bumble-bees tangling their way into the woodbine that has overgrown the graves. The honeysuckle perfume will be heavy in the sunshine. I shall sit there for a long time, thinking about my father and my mother and my Gran who lies nearby, and dreaming of the long-ago summer days in the arbour. *Ilex Lutea. Ilex Lutea.*

Beyond the cemetery the woodland stretches down to the river. In the old days, boys from the village used to bathe there in summertime. We often watched their merriment, my father and I. I was not allowed to bathe because I could not swim and the river is very deep below the graveyard.

One summer, two boys were tragically drowned there, and now no one ever goes. Today, I shall go.

Now I will put this diary in an envelope addressed to you, Doctor. I will mark it personal. I can depend on Sally to give it into your hands.

I hope I have helped you as you tried to help me. And thank you.

Letter from the Past

Rena was not yet accustomed to the run of the studio nor the protocol of the people who ran it. She was acutely conscious of the good luck, at her age, in being asked to do the occasional book review on television. She enjoyed reading the books and writing the critiques. The presenter was a pleasant woman, not so much younger than herself. The producer was less pleasant; he always appeared harried. On his good will depended her continuing good luck. With apprehension she heard him call her name when the session ended and they were drifting out of the room.

"Rena, there is a letter on my desk which may be of interest to you. It was addressed to me, so I opened it."

She followed him into his office. He stood while she read the letter. "I usually drop these things into the waste-paper basket," he told her, "so many of them every day."

She put the letter into her bag. She took a deep breath, and she hoped that her voice would come out strong and steady.

"Thank you, Mr Moroney," she said, "the letter is from an old friend of my late husband. Thank you for saving it for me."

The producer looked gratified. He reached across the desk to pick up two glossy new books. "A bit of a mix," he said, "travel and poetry. Could you do these, say in a fortnight?"

"I would be glad to, Mr Moroney. Thank you again." She was conscious of a double lift in her spirits as she tucked the two books down beside the letter.

Today, Rena made a point of thinking busily about the route home: avoid the city centre, down Leeson Street, across Stephen's Green, through the Liberties, and up the main road of Phoenix Park. If her mind strayed to the letter, she drew it back sharply to concentrating on the car's performance. The old car was a necessity because her country road was not served by a bus now, and the train was a distance away. The television work paid for the car, and again she drew back her thoughts from Mr Moroney to decide on the everyday pick-up of bread and milk in the village which was on the last four miles home.

The journey took almost an hour. The old house among its trees was always a welcome sight. Rena did all the customary things with extra care and attention to postpone the taking-out of the letter, almost as if the letter was an unexpected but never forgotten guest. She set a little tray with a pretty cup and saucer. She put some milk in a pretty little jug. This was definitely not the evening for milk direct from a carton. She made tea in a china pot. She plugged in the electric fire in her bedroom and she carried the tray upstairs. Then at last, she took out the letter:

Dear Mr Moroney,

I enjoy your excellent series of book reviews which comes to London on Sunday morning courtesy of Channel Sixteen. I believe one of your people is an old friend of my family, Rena Grady, and I should like you to convey my congratulations to her on her appearance in your show. It would be a great pleasure to meet her and congratulate her personally when I come to Ireland. Thanking you etc.

Morgan Hayes

Rena liked the discretion of the letter. An old friend of his family indeed! Did he ever mention his family to her? He was Johnny's friend. Johnny had brought Morgan home with him for supper one night in their early married days. Johnny had brought home a long succession of friends, chaps he had gone to school with, fellows he played rugby with, guys from the office. A following of men, Rena thought sadly, right up to the day he died—dozens of them—but only one Morgan.

I can sit here and recall Morgan's memory now, Rena thought. There is no one now to whom I am being unfaithful. So many times in the last thirty years I have had to banish the sudden remembrance, the tug on the heart-strings. Rena held the letter tenderly with her finger-tips. She read it again and again, searching for some single word that would be an index to undo the discretion of the whole. She studied the address in a suburb of London. It yielded no clue as to how well, or how ordinarily, Morgan was housed. Rena had been in London a few times but as to the postal code, that was a mystery. It should be enough satisfaction simply to know that he had written, without searching for a reason. But why, all the same? Why after thirty years? Why after five years since Johnny's death?

Johnny had never mentioned Morgan from the day Morgan went to England. He had gone without coming round to say goodbye, without the usual farewell party, without even the stag booze-up in the local. Just disappeared.

For the very first time, and still holding the letter tenderly, Rena wondered was there a reason for Morgan to be afraid—that is apart from the fact that he had made her pregnant? Now Rena remembered how her guilt forced her silently to rehearse comments on Morgan's sudden flight: Wonder where he got himself to? He could have dropped a line to you, couldn't he, Johnny? We do miss him, don't we? Rena was no actress, and the comments never surfaced. Johnny said nothing so obviously that Rena knew that Johnny was aware. Handsome, charming, happy-go-lucky Johnny was nobody's fool.

Johnny's silence was always hard to take, but his support never faltered. When the children were older, she went back to teaching. Her contribution was acknowledged in the same silent style. It irked, but her own guilt could not redress the balance. She, too, learned to shrug.

In the same way that money burns a hole in the pocket, Morgan's letter burned a hole in Rena's handbag. After three days, she answered, trying to equal his discretion and yet be a little warmer so he would be encouraged to write again:

Dear Morgan,

It was a lovely surprise when Mr Moroney gave me your letter. Thank you for praising the series. As you will see, I am still in the old house, much too big for me since Johnny's death, with the family scattered. The phone is direct-dial even down here now, so if you intend coming out, perhaps you would ring. All the best,

Rena.

When she had posted the letter, it seemed like a pleading invitation which she regretted. Nevertheless, the days seemed endless while she waited and wondered. Had she cut off the need for a reply by carelessly suggesting a phone-call? But surely his letter had been an invitation to initiate a correspondence? When the phone rang, she rushed to it. It was never Morgan, and she felt chagrin at her disappointment. I am not being unfaithful to anyone now, she tried to reassure herself.

When his letter came, she was almost dizzy with excitement. This is silly, she smiled, at my age.

My dear Rena,

Those three little words say it all. Stuck here in England, going through the motions of scratching a living and being a family man, those three words make it all seem so unimportant. My sister came over last year to spend a week with me. Inevitably your name came up, she had seen you on the television. Whatever I said I forget, but she said to me, "Morgan, you are a very lonely man." And I said a peculiar thing, prophetic as it turned out, "The story is not over yet." And here I am, treasuring your letter. Life is good. No classic book-review phrases for me, Rena, but you always were a very special person.

Morgan

This letter took several evenings of sifting and seeking. "Family man" was a different man altogether—perhaps a widower with a grown-up family all left home? And "Prophetic?" Prophecy is to foretell the future, isn't it? Did Morgan imagine a future with Rena?

A future? This was an idea that should concentrate, very precisely indeed, her wavering thoughts.

Rena left the TV books and her notes downstairs. In her bedroom she stood at the window irresolutely gazing out at the trees, old memory blocking out concentration. Into focus had come not the evening he had decided to hook off to England because he had made her pregnant but the evening, four years later, when he had come back from England. That term, "direct-dial," was a subconscious invocation of that very evening. In that time, the phone line went through the local village post-office, and great care was taken not to let the post-mistress into the secrets of life. Morgan had phoned to tell her he was home and wanted to see her that night. Naturally, knowing the tradition, he had disguised his voice, disguised the meeting-place, disguised the time. Still disguised, they had assured and reassured each other that they were perfectly certain of the time and place—perfectly certain.

The futility of that unfulfilled rendezvous was coming back to Rena through the window like an encroaching rain-mist on a lens of self-pity. Suddenly, her attention was caught by a movement in the trees, in the darkening trees along the drive. At first she was puzzled. Then she smiled. The wind was slapping the rope-ladder of the tree-house against the trunk. Johnny had made the tree-house over twenty years ago. He had made it for the little boy who was Morgan's son, and he had made it strong and good. He made many things for that little boy, because he could never give him love. The boy was never discussed nor was the giving of love to him ever discussed. When the boy died in an accident on a school-outing, neither mourning nor remorse was discussed. Quickly, from long practice, that image was banished. Tomorrow, Rena said to herself, I must remember to put the rope-ladder in the shed until the grandchildren come again.

The night of Morgan's disguised phone-call, she had stood in the shelter at the far side of the local park. She had stood for four hours. She could not go home because she was supposed to be visiting a sick aunt who lived in the city. It is possible when you are in your early twenties to hope against hope for four hours. To hope each minute that you have got the message wrong and that Morgan will search other places. After four hours you are still in your twenties, and it is still possible to make ten thousand excuses for someone you love, for someone who is the only person for whom you have ever felt love compounded with desire at once guilty and nerve-wracking and utterly irresistible.

At last, Rena turned away from the window. She

took up Morgan's letter again. Now she gazed lovingly at the appealing words, the words that did not need analysis: "My dear Rena." That *my* meant a lot. Going through the motions—oh, yes, Rena understood that, you can go through the motions for years on end. And "treasuring your letter," *treasuring* was nice. "The story isn't over yet." That meant hope, surely? He hoped there was more to come, more to give. "Always a special person." *Special* had a good ring to it.

Then, as if memory had flipped to reverse, she remembered coming home that night, jaded and frozen. A couple of Johnny's friends were lounging over the fire with him, they were all drinking beer. They stood up to go, "Didn't realise it was so late...better be moving...see you at the club Saturday...oh by the way, saw an old friend of yours earlier tonight...in Fitz's...been drinking all day...he was paralattic!"

"Oh, who was that?" drawled Johnny easily.

"Morgan. Morgan Hayes. 'Member him?"

Johnny said nothing. Nothing at all.

Even now at fifty-six years of age, I can still find excuses why Morgan went off and got drunk. Something that stirs within me understands. She took up her pen:

Dear Morgan,

Just ring when you come, and I'll be over to the station to meet you. The TV stuff is filmed and taped on Mondays. Otherwise, I'll be here.

Rena.

After that, she held her breath and time stood still.

Only clichés can enclose the sort of suspense which floats on air. In a fortnight came a postcard:

Travelling over Thursday 20th. Evening train. M.

So Thursday 20th became a D-Day. She must look her best. The house must look its best. A special meal. The table elegantly set. Wine. Glasses. The good cutlery. Ah, yes, a fire would be welcoming, the evenings had drawn in, it would soon be winter. Would he stay? Perhaps over Christmas? We have an old friend of your father's to stay for Christmas! And her family would say: "Oh Mum, how nice for you!" Old to them was old. The old would never be unconventional.

At 5 p.m. Rena made a last tour of the house. The place had never looked better. She left on all the lights. The house would shine through the gloaming like a Christmas tree. The cosy fire was neatly banked. The Waterford glass gleamed on the table. The subdued cooking-smell was most inviting: the food all ready to take out of the oven, it was merely keeping warm. Her coat and keys were to hand in the hall. The moment he rang from the station, she would jump into the car and speed away to meet him. She caught sight of herself in the long mirror—a fairly pleasing sight—she had not worn so badly. Then the phone rang.

"Rena here."

"Ah, Rena, how nice to hear you!"

"And you, too, Morgan! You are at the station?"

"Yes, my dear. Now there is no need for you to come for us. There is a taxi here to take some packets from the train, and I have arranged with him to come back for us after his delivery. He will be ten minutes only. So, allowing for that, and the run over, we should be there in less than half an hour! How is that, my dear?"

Rena took the receiver from her ear and stared at it. Us? We? And his voice was kind of fruity.

"Oh, Morgan, are you there?"

"Yes, my dear, we are here."

"How many of you *are* there, Morgan?"

"Just my wife and I, Rena dear. We are making a little holiday of it. We are just now going to have a teensy G and T while we are waiting for the taxi. Bye, my dear, for the moment!"

He had put down the phone!

Rena did not take time for clichés like bursting the bubble and going up in smoke. Two basins of water doused the cosy fire effectively. The electric oven was switched off. A run through the house and all lights were gone. She checked there were no windows open, and she bolted the back door securely. She snatched up her coat and her keys. Out on the front steps, she thought she heard the sound of a car engine on the long hill. It just might be the taxi so there was no time to get her own car out of the garage and drive off. The taxi-man would recognise her car if she passed him, he might even reverse and follow, thinking she had misunderstood. She ran towards the trees to hide. Suddenly she remembered the rope-ladder. Within minutes she was up in the tree-house, and she pulled up the rope-ladder.

The car on the long hill puttered away into the distance, to be replaced by the straining noise of Dermody's old taxi. The taxi headlights illuminated the scene for her from her tree-top shelter.

The completely darkened house was, blatantly, a

shock to the three people who got out of the taxi, and stared up at it. Dermody proceeded to take out his passengers' suitcases, and carry them up the steps to the hall door. The stout man was knocking on the door, and even shouting through the letter-box.

"That is Morgan," Rena was musing sadly, "but he is not my Morgan. My Morgan was tall and blond and he walked like a prince."

The stout man who was Morgan directed Dermody, the taxi-man, to walk around the house to the back. Dermody obeyed, bellowing as he went: "Not a wisp of smoke! Not a sound of any sort! The missus must be up above in the city! She goes regular up to the city! She be's on the television!"

There was more shouting and calling and instructing. At last, the three people got into the taxi, and Dermody drove them away. Rena was profoundly grateful that the stout Morgan man had not dismissed the taxi at the start. A tree-house was only for small children. She listened carefully until she heard the taxi toil up the long hill. She longed to go back into the house and eat the going-cold savoury chicken-casserole in the snug comfort of her own bed. More than that, much more than that, she longed never to have to look on the face of that stout Morgan man should he choose to return in daylight.

Very gingerly, she descended the rope-ladder. This was not the time to break an ankle. This was get-away time in case the visitors had second thoughts. Swiftly she drove the car out of the garage, rapidly she locked the double doors. She looked regretfully up at the house, but only for a second. Once in the car, and moving smoothly down the drive, a light-hearted sense of accomplishment took over. It was a sense of averting danger, of regaining control, of being back safely in her own body.

Where would a middle-aged lady go at nightfall? A middle-aged lady without luggage? Without a cheque-book? Without a credit-card? Where but to the home of a married daughter some sixty miles further west. And what explanation would the middle-aged lady give to her daughter?

"Just a notion I took, Trassa!"

Good-looking Trassa never questioned people's notions. She would give her mother that long, familiar, lazy look from under her thick eyelashes. She would never think to comment. She was the one in the family who most took after Johnny.

Framed in Silver

The first day young John Carlin had come to the house, the picture was there, standing on the piano. He had been shown into the drawing-room to await Miss MacDara, the landlady. At once he noticed the piano and he hoped he would be allowed use it. Then he saw the picture in its ornate silver frame: a studio photograph of a young woman with a baby in her arms.

The landlady was not old, into the thirties perhaps, but she had an oldish way of solemn dignity. To a twenty-two-year-old man on his first incursion into the working-world, she seemed to belong to another generation.

"Sister Conleth phoned me to say that you are new to the town, and need a room?" He would come to know that she used direct speech with the minimum of words.

"I am teaching music and mathematics in the convent, from September," he replied. "If you have no room, perhaps you could recommend..."

"I have a room," she said quietly. "I will show it to you." His ear caught an accent that was not of the midland town. Derry? Donegal?

They went upstairs. It was a clean, uncluttered house. The room was sparsely furnished. The woman stood silently at the door while he walked over to the window. On the other side of the road were trees, and far in the distance he could see the Keeper Mountains.

"I like the room," he said. "I would need a breakfast and an evening meal."

"They would be served in the dining-room. I have two other lodgers, men also. One of them opened the door for you."

"Teachers?" he asked.

"They are in the office of the new factory," she replied.

"Sister Conleth told me what the rent is," he murmured, suddenly shy about his first earnings.

"Is it all right?" Even with a question, her voice did not rise in interrogation.

"Yes, thank you." He tried to match her even tones, to show no enthusiasm, to be very adult. "I will be going home to Athlone most weekends."

She held open the hall door. Now he hesitated. From where he stood in the hall, he could see the piano and the silver-framed picture. "Do you allow your...er...er...paying-guests to play your piano?"

Her eyes followed his gaze. He thought her eyes lingered on the scene. "Provided other lodgers do not object," she said.

"Thank you," he said, out on the garden path. She shut the door gently. Lodgers? Paying-guests? She saw a difference evidently, and she took comfort from that difference.

John Carlin moved in at the end of August. Miss MacDara had added a desk and an electric fire to the furniture in his room. The electric fire had a meter. He felt very independent and quite mature, marking his class papers at his desk, preparing his class notes for next day, and warming his toes at his electric fire. When he heard the other lodgers going out to the local pub for their nightly pints, he switched off the fire, and went down to the piano in the now empty drawing-room.

Seating himself at the piano, he would examine the photograph in the polished silver frame. It seemed he caught the girl's eyes happily returning his salute, extending to him the tenderness implicit in the way she held her baby. His hands wandered over the keyboard while his eyes locked into the eyes of the girl. The music came very softly as if whispering against her pretty hair.

In his second year, John went out to teach piano to pupils in their homes. His fame as a good teacher spread. He acquired a car. In his third year, he formed a small dance band. In a year or two, the band became one of the Big Bands. The car was replaced by a white mini-bus. He gave up teaching. The text-books were packed in cartons and sent to his parents' home in Athlone.

Strangely he never thought of leaving his lodging in the small country town, that room with its desk and its electric meter and its view of the Keeper Mountains. He could be away for several weeks, then again would come a night when the piano in the drawing-room would echo softly to his love-notes. Although the landlady scarcely spoke when he returned, the girl in the picture welcomed him back. He could almost feel the soft contour of her face against his closed eyes. The dance-band life yielded plenty of girls on plenty of nights but none with enough interest to hold him.

He was thirty-two years of age when his mother died. Her death was followed swiftly by the death of his father, who could not accept the loss of his life's partner. John's sisters were younger than he, both married and occupied with young families. There were many arrangements to be made before John was able to take up his own work again. He returned to his quiet landlady.

"Would you like me to pack for you?" Miss MacDara asked when she had sympathised, briefly, on his parents' deaths.

"Are you asking me to leave?" Then he added harshly, "Throwing me out after all these years?"

She turned her head away from him. She did not speak for a moment. Then she said in her low voice, "You are welcome to stay." She went out of the room, half-closing the door.

John sat down at the piano. The girl in the silver frame was waiting for him. Her palpable tenderness drew his eyes to hers, to her throat, to the barely defined outline of her young breast. He closed his eyes on the unbidden thought of the baby at her breast, as so recently he had witnessed his sister feeding her new baby, the tears rolling down her face because of death. Soft-pedalling, John told his sorrow. He and his sisters had cared deeply for their parents. In his heart, he had cried for the childish weeping of the little grandchildren who could not understand why Gran and Grandad had gone to heaven without telling them.

You console me, he told the girl in the picture. Please be there for me always. Your eyes are glistening for my grief.

John knew his landlady was in the kitchen,

preparing the evening meal. For the first time in all the years he had lived in the house, he went down the hall, down the three steps and opened the door to the kitchen. She was standing by the window as if lost in thought.

"I am sorry," he said, "I should not have spoken like that."

She did not turn, nor answer.

"Are you all right?"

"I was listening to your music," her voice was barely a whisper.

From the door, John said quickly, "Will you marry me?"

She put her hands over her face. "Will you marry me?" he repeated in a louder voice.

Now she looked at him. Was it pity in her face, or was it fear? An instinct told him that she would defer his request, and he knew he would accept her deferral. His acceptance of her terms would be his personal sacrifice for this enigmatic shadow woman.

"You must go away," she said. There was no regretful sweetness in her tone. For him, there would never be. "You have been through a severe crisis. You know that."

"Yes," he said firmly, "And now it is over."

"Also, you are too young," she said, "and you are too handsome."

"I am thirty-two." He had raised his voice again.

"And I shall soon be forty," she answered evenly. "Your life has not yet begun." She was turning away from him. He crossed the room. She had not said the word of refusal. He touched her hand. "So we will marry," he said.

The marriage took place. His sisters supported

him loyally at the wedding, turning it into a joyful occasion, their husbands teasingly accusing him of "hanging up his hat." His bride was placid and submissive, lovely in a remote sort of loveliness. If she had thoughts, they were veiled. John had planned the honeymoon in Paris. As a student, he had worked his summers in France. Paris was for lovers. Paris, he hoped, was not for inhibitions.

Marian accepted his love-making. As he had known, she was a woman to defer. The couple of weeks were a break, a holiday from routine, but never the honeymoon John had dreamed. And yet, in due course their only child was born. She named him Thomas.

John prospered. There was no need for paying-guests. The rooms of the house filled up with carpets and pictures and flowers. John toured with his band; he managed other musicians; he published and recorded his own songs. He was often away for weeks at a time. The bedroom with its view of the Keeper Mountains remained his special sanctum. When he sought his wife's double bed, she was acquiescent and coldly tender. Her words for him were few and direct, but never aggressive, never argumentative. Her life centred obsessively on their only child.

Marian and the boy Thomas. He was hers. She was his. That was clear from the beginning—in the house, in the world.

Whatever an occasional dance-floor girl might offer John, he always returned to his wife and his son. The woman who welcomed him home was the one in the silver frame. Rapturously holding her baby, she was ready for his fingers on the keys forever harmonising her heart and his.

For twenty-four years, the only changes in the routine of John's married life were wrought by Thomas's childhood, his adolescence, his growing into a man. Quiet and clever, he sailed through schooldays into college and out of it. With his first-class degree he went to an American university for a Master's degree in economics. While working towards a doctorate, he accepted the offer of an excellent position in Detroit.

Now Marian seemed prepared to thrive on phone-calls and the regular letter. To John it was a constant affirmation that his wife and their son were enclosed in their own self-sufficient world. He assured himself that their exclusive preoccupation with each other was a fulfilling of their natures which he would never presume to question, and certainly never to resent. If he had allowed himself the faint hope that Thomas's departure to Detroit would change anything, he came to know it would not.

In the summer Thomas brought home an American girl. John gave Thomas his second car, and the young couple went off touring. In the autumn, the letters from Detroit became full of Kathy. Their wedding was planned for the following Easter. John and Marian would make the trip to Detroit for the event. He would like to have known, but he did not know, whether his wife was pleased or vexed? As in every other matter, she kept her own counsel in her cool, but not unfriendly, fashion.

Early in December, Marian died suddenly. John had gone to the post-office with her Christmas cards and her presents for Kathy and Kathy's family. Cerebral haemorrhage, the doctors said, but John knew better. Marian's life-work was completed when Thomas went.

Father and son had never confided in each other. John longed to share his grief. He encountered a cold resentment. He was unable to say that he felt bitterly Marian's instruction in her will that she be interred in the grave of her parents in far-off Donegal. He wanted to know if Thomas's markedly resentful attitude had to do with the willing of the house to his father for his lifetime. Thomas would inherit on John's death. Since John was now fifty-six, Thomas could wait a long time. John thought to alter that.

On the night before the funeral, when the last mourning neighbour had gone, John built up the fire in the drawing-room and set out another bottle of whiskey.

"There is a matter I want to discuss," he said to Thomas. "Draw up your chair. Is that your glass? Perhaps we could…?"

Thomas, glaring, interrupted him. "Make it fast, Father. I still have jet-lag, and I don't drink whiskey. I am going to bed. Tomorrow will be a long day. Donegal!"

"Yes, I know," and John paused. Strange, he thought, how my son is always more adult than I am. "About the house," he began again, "You will be needing to buy a place in Detroit very soon. I am quite willing to vacate this so you can sell it and…that is, of course, if you wish. I mean, what I mean is that it would be more useful to you now rather than…"

Thomas stood up to his full height. His voice was cold as he spaced out the words. "My mother's wishes will be respected by me. She wished you to have this place. She always said so."

And that, John thought, is the direct speech your mother would use. Terse. That terseness had always made him hesitant. It was no surprise to him that Thomas knew Marian's wishes.

"Well, er, I, er, would, er, like," he made an effort to control his voice, "If there is anything I can, or you..."

Thomas was ready with his answer to all the unspoken questions, "Mother told me also that you had bought everything that is of value in the house. It is all yours, she said. I will take my mother's picture and nothing else."

Thomas crossed the room to the piano, and taking the silver frame in his hands, he looked deeply into the eyes of the girl in the photograph. John could scarcely breathe. His throat choked on angry protests. It was a second death when Thomas walked out of the room, taking the picture with him.

John's sisters and their husbands stood with him and Thomas at the graveside. There were a few local people, old friends and old neighbours of Marian's family. John cordially asked that they come back for a meal to the hotel. Snow was beginning to fall. Everyone bundled into cars. John started the engine, the silent Thomas seated beside him.

"Those two old men look in need of a lift. They were at the grave," John indicated the old men who were setting out to walk. "Will I stop?"

Thomas was indifferent. "It is your car. Stop if you want to."

John pulled up, and rolled down the window. "Will ye not be coming back to the hotel?" he asked invitingly.

The old men looked like twin brothers, equally weather-bent and wrinkled. "Yerra no, but thanks forbye. We are eight miles out the road, and a few sheep to round in. 'Twould be away out of your road."

"Not at all," John said, "the snow is settling down. Hop in there."

The old men scrambled into the back seats, commenting on the grand comfort of it all. John had a flask of whiskey and he passed it back to them. They took great slurps, gesturing to pass it back.

"Finish it, let ye," said John. "You were good to come so far on such a bad day." They slurped again. One of them leaned forward and tapped Thomas on the shoulder.

"You would be Marian MacDara's son, would you, sir?"

Thomas glanced back, "I am." His short manner would not encourage communication. The old men did not notice.

Firmly holding onto the flask, one of them said, "We were watching you at the grave, God bless you, and we didn't think you looked into the thirties? But the MacDaras never showed their age. I knew you for a MacDara. Small trace of Thomas O'Donnell in your looks, begor!"

"I am Thomas Carlin," said Thomas more civilly. "My mother was Marian MacDara."

"Carlin? Carlin?" repeated the old man. "Thomas Carlin O'Donnell? 'Tis a mouthful! And your mother, so, was Marian MacDara O'Donnell. Her father was Maurice MacDara, our Uncle Maurice; she was his only girsha; the mammy died when Marian was a small *leanbh*. Less than a year, she was. Wasn't that right, Mikey?"

"We all went to school here in Ardara, us cousins," Mikey said, "but Thomas O'Donnell was from Gweedore, north of Gweedore, wasn't he?"

"He was so, and they were married here in Ardara."

"I knew the lad was a MacDara, he is the spit out of his grandfather, our Uncle Maurice."

Thomas was not given to suffering fools. He turned to the back of the car. "I am Thomas Carlin. You are confused."

"Divil the confused!" and they both slurped at the flask. "Your mother and Thomas O'Donnell went to America within days of the wedding. We heard here in Ardara about the fire, but wouldn't you have all that knowledge yourself. Glory to God that you were spared to your mother, God rest her and she gone on the way of truth. And there you are, the very spit out of the MacDaras."

"She was only out of the Convent School the day she was married to Thomas O'Donnell from Gweedore. Was she seventeen, Mikey?"

"If that itself! A very quiet girl, and reckoned a great good-looker, may she rest peaceful. We were good people, decent stock, the MacDaras. Turn by the left here, sir. We're a couple of mile up the way but the road is washed out. From north of Gweedore Thomas O'Donnell's people were, wasn't that right, Mikey? There's a good wide place for you to turn your vehicle, sir."

The old men, climbing upwards, were lost in the swirling snow. John Carlin's imagination cast about wildly, vainly, hopelessly, for the magic words that would blot out the meanderings of the old brothers. The meanderings had the ring of truth...two old men living in a rickle of these stony mountains, arguing over times and dates of long ago, and never dreaming that they had brought a world crashing down. John cleared his throat. "My sisters are staying overnight in Ballyshannon. I asked them to book us into the hotel. This is no weather for travelling."

Thomas did not speak.

John had plenty of time to think on the long road back to the shelter of the Keeper Mountains. An unexpected memory brought back Marian's smile when she knew that a birth certificate and a photo were sufficient for the passport to Paris. Yes, the MacDaras were quiet people. He had listened to Marian's silence for thirty-five years, and now he listened to Thomas's.

Until they were back in the house.

Then the storm broke. John was switching on all the heat when Thomas came down the stairs. He was carrying the picture in the silver frame. The hatred in his face was malignant. He thrust the picture at his father.

"You knew, didn't you! All these years you knew! You let me make a fool of myself. You never spoke. Parading my name in front of those stinking old men! Smiling to yourself as you always do—self-satisfied—purse-proud!"

Thomas's voice almost broke. His father stood back sadly, listening to thoughts revealed that he had never known. Self-satisfied? If you only knew, my son. And purse-proud? He had never withheld, never grudged, a pound of his considerable earnings. Should he tell Thomas that the picture was there on the piano when he was younger than

Thomas was now. Marian had never referred to the picture in the silver frame. He had respected her silence. Marian's silence was Marian. It did not help him to know now that her silence included Thomas, her idol.

"Take it! Take it!" Thomas shouted at him, his eyes blazing. He pushed the picture into his father's hands. The front door banged resoundingly. Thomas had gone into the snow.

John felt very tired. He sat down at the fire with the picture in his hands. He had never held it before. It was an act of intimacy, at once too tenuous and too final. He folded his arms across the picture and, after a while, he fell into a light sleep through which he was dimly conscious of waiting, as he had always waited, for Marian's step in the hall.

When the front door slammed open, John went out to meet his son, grateful that he had come home. Thomas was kicking the snow off his shoes, and struggling out of his heavy coat. His movements were unsteady. Thomas who never drank more than a glass of wine, Thomas whose normal manner was of cold dignity, this same Thomas had tried to drown his problems in the local pub. He missed the rack with his first attempt to hang his coat.

"Thomas," John began diffidently, and holding out the picture, "Thomas, this is…"

Thomas made as if to brush his father aside. "I don't want it," he said thickly. "It means nothing. Who is she, anyway? Your precious room is full of pictures of your singing girls! Your famous bands! You were the great photographer—the latest and greatest camera from Japan! How could I know that you did not take that picture of my mother and me?

Your room is full of framed pictures of young girls—dozens of them. Framed in silver had to be the special one. That's what I thought—more fool me!"

Halfway up the stairs, he turned and glared again at his father, "So there is no picture of me and my mother. That's the picture you never bothered to take! Always your singing girls—never my mother and me!"

John began to speak. He held out the picture. He started up the stairs, but Thomas would have none of him. "Keep it!" he roared, "Keep it! I don't give a curse who it is! I don't want it! Keep it!"

The bedroom door was banged to shake the house, and John heard Thomas slumping heavily onto his bed. He hesitated on the stairs for a long time. He had never been a man to intrude on the closed door, the forbidding silence, the lowered eyelids. He had learned to stay away, to wait for the sun to rise again. It had not been easy to learn.

The next morning, they drove to Shannon for Thomas's flight back to America. They neither spoke nor embraced. They did not even say the words of goodbye.

In the late evening, John lit the fire in the drawing-room. He thought to assuage the loneliness of the house. Sadly he supposed that now he would have to hire people to keep in good order the house and land that would someday go to Thomas.

He went into the kitchen, taking the picture with him. He found a small screwdriver and very gently he removed the silver frame. He examined the uncovered photograph. There was a photographer's name: Benny Stein, Montauk, Long Island. Written neatly on the photograph were the words: Marian and Baby Thomas O'Donnell at 3 months.

Carefully, John polished the glass and the silver frame. He put in the picture and replaced the back. Then, as if bearing the Holy Sacrament, he carried his treasure back to its accustomed place on the piano.

Touching the keyboard softly, he looked at her. Did I always know, he mused. Right from the very beginning of my loving her, did I know that you, my love, had vanished into my silent landlady? I had guessed long and long before she said: I was listening to your music. What phantoms came out of my music into her mind? And when she listened, was she aware of the passion she aroused in me? When I held in my arms my coldly tender wife, I knew that deep within her was a sensuality imprisoned by some mysterious tragedy... imprisoned in a silver frame. I knew, oh yes I knew and I hoped. I never stopped hoping.

The piano was giving back a lonely melody in phrases of hopeless regret. Of course I knew. That day I came home unexpectedly. She was feeding my little son by this fireside. I got the camera. I wanted that picture of them, the two of them there, the flowers on the table, the lacy shawl. She drew the shawl across her naked bosom, and she hurried away to another room. I knew for certain then. There was something in the way she held our baby, just as you do, my darling. Something in the way her hair fell against her cheek, the tender curve of her cheek.

He drew his fingers lingeringly along the length of the keyboard. Thomas O'Donnell, wherever you are now, you had the best of it then.

A Bit of a Playboy

D es had waited in Westland Row station since the early morning boat-train. He knew, because he had made careful phone-calls, that Inez, his wife, left her office in time for the five o'clock train. Everyone, he was told, went for the five o'clock train, no one could get petrol for private motoring.

"Are the trains on time?" he asked the porter.

"It's easy seein' you've been away!" The porter eyed Des's lone suitcase and shabby duffle bag with an experienced eye that foretold of no profit. "Were yeh over the water? Youse are all comin' home now the war is over!"

"Did you go yourself?" asked Des, entering into the Dublin jargon with a long-missed familiarity.

"Ah now," grinned the porter, "Someone had to stay and mind the bloody country!"

"And what about the trains?" pursued Des.

"Few and far between, mister. We're scalded from them! They run when they feel like it!"

"Is it the scarcity of man-power, or the scarcity of coal?"

"Coal, is it?" and the porter spat out an oath. "Coal? Sure they save that for the long distance. These local lads is run on turf!"

"Turf?" echoed Des, only half-believing the Dublin wit.

"And wet turf at that! If yeh don't get on the five, mister, there's one more between seven and eight. Good luck to yeh!"

Des pressed a half-note into the porter's willing hand, and saw him head for the station bar. Des could anticipate the porter's order to the bar-man: "a quick one!" And Des knew the perfection of "a quick one": the immediate elixir-like taste on the palate with the arousing anticipation of the long, dark, creamy draught to follow: the quick one and the chaser. So well did Des know! It was safer not to remember after his two years of total abstinence.

He went to the station cafe for tea and a sandwich. He took a seat near a window and kept an eye on people coming up the steps. The hands of the station clock were moving towards three o'clock. When the window misted, he rubbed a viewing space with his cuff.

Inez knew the station would be crowded. On Friday the station was always crowded. On Friday, the emigrants either went on the boat to England, or they came home from England when the overtime was good. Thousands went, and thousands never came back. England had endured a lengthy war, and now in England there was full employment with overtime. The dead heroes had left room for emigrants. On every Friday, Inez thought the self-same thoughts as she pushed her way up the steps, wedged among hundreds.

On the platform the crowd was dense. Still pushing Inez joined in the struggle towards the train. Suddenly, her arm was grabbed and she was swung round, almost losing her balance. Furiously, she struck a hand from her arm, her angry eyes shafting upwards. It was her husband.

Her instant rejection was in her appraising glance: an emigrant from England's war, wearing dusty emigrant clothes. She disdained him as if she had never seen him. She resumed the struggle for the train, and he resumed his grip. He had to shout to make her hear him. He wanted to plead, but he had to shout.

"Inez, I have to talk to you—Inez!" He could feel the stiff, obdurate resistance as she pressed away from him.

"Inez—can't you give me five minutes—Inez!"

She almost broke loose from his grasping fingers. She had nearly reached the train.

"Mum! Mum!" It was a pretty young woman, clutching a little child and a mass of parcels.

Defeated, Inez stumbled backwards. It was Lyn, her daughter. Only Lyn would venture into town on a Friday with a child and a load of shopping. The struggle closed behind Inez and she was swept back to the barricade, her husband still clinging to her arm.

Lyn set down the little child. Looking up at her mother, she saw the man beside her.

"Oh my God," she cried, "Is it my daddy?" She hugged him, but very briefly when she saw her mother's face. "Daddy, this is Clara."

Des knelt down beside the tiny girl. He knew her for his grandchild. She had his brown eyes, no mistake, and they had given her his mother's name, Clara. His grandchild. It was a moment of such wonder as he had never known.

"Hello, Clara. How old are you?"

"I am not old," she said in a small clear voice, "I am three." She reached for her mother's hand. In the other hand she carried a little handbag. Des pulled money from his pocket, and tried to put it in the handbag which she promptly put behind her back.

"No," she piped, "Mummy says never take money from strangers."

Des stood up. Lyn was trying to say something but her mother's eyes stopped her with the hostility of their message: Yes, he is a stranger. I hope that stings him like a whip on a wound.

"Inez, I have got to speak to you."

"And we have to get on this train, Lyn—come, the crowd is thinning. This could be the last train. Hurry, give me the parcels, you take up Clara, and we will push together. Hurry, Lyn!"

"Inez, I will come too, I want to…"

"No!" the woman screamed at him. "No!"

Tears rushed into Lyn's eyes, "Daddy, you can come to my house…" They were still all plunging forward together although he had been refused. "No, Lyn, no…my own house…I…"

Inez, almost obscured by parcels, had gained a foothold and she pulled up Lyn against other people, and across Lyn's shoulder, she shot the words at him: "Your house! Not any more!"

The crowd swept aside his faltering hesitation, and in a split second the compartment was packed to overflowing. He could barely see his grandchild's bright hair against Lyn's sad face.

When the train pulled out of the station, all Des Ferguson's plans went for naught. Damn and blast, he thought savagely, I could have gone home on an earlier train instead of hanging around this dump all day. After all, I still have my own door-key. Unless my stony-faced wife has changed the lock. In which event, I'll bang the door down. If she would only listen to me...He walked up and down the now empty platform. The passengers who were stranded had all sought comfort in the bar.

God dammit, Des thought, I would have handled that encounter with more class if I had tucked four whiskeys under my belt. Abstinence my foot!

He pushed open the door of the bar and stood on the threshold. Like a breath of life came the shouting male voices, every shining face a reflection of his own thirst, silvery cigarette smoke curling seductively, the whiskey-laden fragrance giving off good cheer like Christmas. Ah, this was the welcome home he had longed for and been denied. Here are friends, he thought.

Inez and her daughter exchanged scarcely a word on the journey. Little Clara, surrounded by huddling strangers, put her arms around Lyn's neck and hid her face in Lyn's collar.

Beyond the aureole of Clara's curls, Lyn could see her mother's set, grim face. Her mother was not always easy to please but not always grim either. Lyn felt guilty because of the way love for her father rushed into her heart the very moment she saw him. Even after all these years. She had always loved him best: he was easy to love. And she had always felt guilty.

Lyn remembered her mother taking her to her grandmother's house to report that Des had left home. That was on Lyn's sixteenth birthday. He had given her a huge box of chocolates that morning. She still had the box. It had a picture of the Alps with skiers and chalets. Her grandmother who was her Daddy's mother had treated the matter rather lightly (or so her mother said later), "Oh, Inez, I shouldn't worry if I were you! Des will be back. You know he was always a bit of a playboy!"

Lyn had asked her mother where had Daddy gone. Her mother's answer was short and bitter: "On the boat to England." So Lyn asked her grandmother: why would Daddy go to England? There must be more exciting places to go, like Monte Carlo? Her grandmother thought he had probably gone off to the war! What war? Her grandmother told her she was a big dunce, didn't she know that England was having a war with Germany? They had one before, about twenty-five years ago, and now they were having another. Her grandmother made it sound rather harmless. Lyn wondered if Daddy would be let join in, seeing as he was Irish…? She remembered her grandmother's wry, sad smile. Lyn's eyes filled with tears. Grandmother was dead now. She had left her house and all its contents to Lyn and what money she had to Lyn's Mum. If grandmother's handsome son, fighting in England's war, knew of the death, he gave no sign. Poor Daddy.

When the train pulled in to Monkstown, Inez snapped at Lyn, "How, in God's name, are you going to manage these parcels and the child?" But Lyn only shook her head. She knew her husband would come down to the station, and as soon as Alan would take Clara from her, her shaky world would settle down again.

Now Inez got a seat in the compartment. Her irritation with Lyn drained away to be replaced by the surging sense of outrage held back while she stood clutching Lyn's parcels. To be accosted in a public station by the husband she had not seen for seven years. How could Lyn kiss that man? Lyn was a softy. Lyn's eyes filled with tears all too easily. Tears for a father who had deserted her? Did Lyn ever stop to think who went out to work to put her through college? Who slaved—yes, slaved—to pay for her expensive education. And for what end? Did Lyn get a job and pay her mother back? Did she? Oh, not Lyn! She married a college professor with all his classy relations. Wedding of the Year, they called it! And who paid for all? So much for the little legacy—every penny of it went on that wedding. And so Lyn, and the elegant Alan, lived in the lovely old house in Monkstown...the house that should, by right, have gone to Des...while she, the deserted wife, struggled to pay the building society for the house she had gone into as a bride.

Seven years. England's war was over now quite a while. At times, she had thought he must be dead. Was he ever in the war at all? She had never got the wife's allowance. Nor any other allowance. A "fancy woman" got it, she supposed—and he was never short of one. She urged on all the bitter thoughts which had kept her incensed in the lonely hours when tears had ceased to flow, and anger was the only comfort.

Inez had a long walk up the hill from Sandycove station. Anger and hatred were a heavy burden, her steps dragged, her head ached. Emptiness was the core of her life if she must go on from day to day. Most of all, expel memory out of the mind. Do not take it into the empty house.

In the neat kitchen, she opened the fridge. Unseeing, she gazed into it. Then she shut it. She filled the electric kettle but she did not plug it in. Vaguely, she decided she was not hungry.

She went into the front room. She switched on a table lamp. The room looked comfortable. She turned on the radio. She had no interest in what she heard. Perhaps she should go to bed. Feeling so jaded, surely tonight she would sleep? There were so many nights when sleep would not come that she had begun to fear going to bed. Sometimes, she read for hours and next day she could not remember what she read.

Inez took off her shoes, and sat on the edge of the bed. She tried to think of what had happened in Westland Row station. The crowds, the little bright-haired child who would not take money from a stranger, the man who offered the money had brown, brown, brown eyes with long curling lashes: a beloved face now a little worn, but the same face. The face had disappeared into a milling throng of people...a receding image of a face that could come back only in a dream, a sad recurring dream.

On the table beside the bed, there was a bottle of codeine tablets, and a glass jug of water. The codeine was there to take care of the headache after a sleepless night. She opened the bottle, two or three would cure her headache now, and she would rest for a while.

She took the tablets with slow sips of water: one, two, three, four, five, six...She emptied out the glass jug. Counting the tablets was like a game, a childish bravado, but at last she lay down.

* * * * *

Des got well up in front of the crowd. He was ready and set to board the last train, and he got a seat in a carriage full of men.

He had stood at the door of the station bar for one long moment. Then he had stepped backward. He occupied the time by finding a place to wash and change his clothes. How could Inez guess that the unshaven emigrant was not off the overnight trip from London to Dun Laoire. He had come from Ceylon, hazardously, without a proper stop, without a look in the mirror. He wanted to explain, but how could she guess?

In the train, he was gathering his forces for the last-ditch effort. If she would let him speak? If she would only listen? That had always been the trouble. He could not explain, express contrition, climb down. And she would not listen anyway.

There had been other women. Faithless as he was faithless. But he could talk to them. Well, the talk was a load of balderdash—a load of fun—a load of silly laughter. He never went silent the way he did with Inez. And yet, without being able to find the way to say it, he longed for her presence in his life...her uprightness, her loyalty, the clean, neat cut of her. Seeing her in Westland Row station, he had fallen in love with her all over again, as if she were new in his life: the slightly foreign look she had inherited from a Spanish grandmother, the wide-spaced eyes and childish mouth, the remembrance of her first kisses.

The loyalty to principles which had so attracted him in the beginning because he was so lacking in it ...*that* he wanted...those qualities back in his own life now that he knew their value. Surely Inez would value the abstinence and utter faithfulness of the past few years...if she would hear him out. Surely she would understand that it had not been easy.

He was still trying to rehearse his opening speech when he arrived at his own front door. His key fitted the lock, the door swung smoothly open. He stood, giving her time to come out into the hall from the front room where the radio was playing country music. The kitchen was lit, it was empty, there was no sign of a recent meal.

Des went into the front room, and turned off the radio. He stood at the foot of the stairs and called her name, softly at first and then a little louder.

Suddenly anxious, Des ran up the stairs. In one swift look he took in the figure on the bed, the bottle, the glass. Within seconds, he had found the telephone directory, the number of the local hospital, and conveyed the urgency of his message. Do nothing, he was told, an ambulance and a doctor would be there as fast as possible. Important, move nothing.

He stood, looking down at her. He longed to touch her hand but he was afraid to disobey the order. He could not tell if she was breathing, there was not a quiver, although her eyes were not fully closed. Something about the relaxed softness of her lying gave him a little hope. Her utter loneliness in the big, double bed brought a desolate lump to his throat. She was small and thin like a child, and, like a child, the corners of her lips were turned down in a little pout.

The clanging of the ambulance sent him racing down the stairs to open the door, his heart pounding with fresh hope. There was no time for questions and answers. Hospital was the place for questions.

Inez was lifted onto a stretcher, the young doctor held an oxygen mask over her face, and she was borne away. The doctor took the codeine bottle in his pocket.

"No, you cannot come in the ambulance. Regulations. Unless in the case of death."

Des hesitated about phoning his mother—so much shock, so many explanations. His mother was in the late seventies now. At last, he took up the phone.

It was Lyn who answered. She listened to his broken voice. Her sympathy was very sweet to him, charged with tears, she repeated in each pause, "Poor Daddy." When he broke down, Lyn took over. "Daddy, we will be with you in fifteen minutes. We will get a taxi. Daddy, suppose you have a quick change...and—are you nodding your head?...please wait there for me...Daddy...I..."

Des replaced the receiver very gently. He was seeing Lyn as the tiny little girl who was Lyn so many years ago, and the tiny little girl at the station who would not take any money from a stranger. Quite right, little girl, a stranger.

He walked up the stairs to put out the bedroom light. The gleaming bathroom stood open as if to invite his weary body. He switched off the lights, every one.

In the hall, he picked up his duffle bag, and suitcase. When he slammed shut the front door, he stood for a moment. Then he dropped his door-key back through the letter-box.

The Golden
Handshake

On the morning of his retirement, Hugh Davan dressed with care. His suit had been purchased recently for his daughter's wedding, his tie had a silvery thread which matched the silvery strands in his still-thick hair. He admired his hair, he was proud of it and of his trim figure. If he had been asked the secret of these youthful attributes, he would have admitted it was the regular game of golf. When Falvey argued that balding men with great paunches also played golf, Hugh did not bother to answer. Falvey did not play golf, so what would he know? He was among the lesser mortals.

The Regular Game of Golf, that was the daily drift of his thoughts. As he drove for the last time from his suburban home to his office, he reviewed the days ahead. His pension would be small but he would be able to keep up the golf. He had arranged to buy a Life-Membership in the golf club, to be paid for out of the lump sum coming to him today. A couple of new irons could be afforded as well. He would salt the rest away for an emergency. An emergency dear to his heart would be a trip on the team to St Andrew's or even further afield for one of the really big events! Of course, the upkeep of the car would come out of the emergency fund—the car was essential for the regular game.

Ah, he would be all right. He had secured a small part-time job, to keep the wolf from the door as you might say. There were only two mouths now to feed. He was lucky to be getting a lump sum. In the old days, lump sums were unheard of. Of course, it could have been a bigger lump sum for all his years of service. Falvey referred to it as a golden handshake in his most sarcastic tone, and told everyone in the office that it was better than a slap in the belly with a wet fish. Falvey was a great reader, and felt free to use language he had not coined for himself. After today, Hugh Davan would not miss Falvey.

Davan was pleased to find that he was first in this morning. It kept his record unbroken. He had completed his work-schedule and tidied his desk. Now he sat reading his *Irish Times*, or pretending to. His thoughts were back in the usual place. The office presentation would take place at midday, and his cheque would be conveyed to him. He would lodge that in the bank, and go home to lunch. The weather looked as perfect for a game of golf as it could possibly look. Maybe he would have dinner in the golf club tonight, treat a few old pals!

"Hugh Davan! You look gorgeous! I never saw that suit on you before! You're like a film star! Look at that tie—is it Italian? Show me! Let me feel it…"

This was Teena. Teena shared her dubious typing skills between himself and Falvey. Now she perched herself up on his desk to examine his tie. Secretly, Davan regarded her as his secretary since Falvey was a recent addition to the staff. Teena had come as a seventeen-year-old and now she was twenty two. In the beginning, she was in much awe of Mr Davan. He had been patient with her spelling, overlooked her poor time-keeping, gave her good reports, secured a bonus for her at Christmas. She played on him, and he indulged her. When Falvey came, and his coming Davan recognised as the beginning of his own end, he had become possessive of Teena. When Falvey threw back her sloppy typing, she came weeping to Davan. Giving her protection, albeit in his sportsmanlike way, had come to fulfil an emotional, perhaps a sensual, need in Davan. When the coarse Falvey muttered, "How do you stand that one in her skimpy skirt up on top of your desk? Where's your hot blood, man!" Davan was able to reply with much dignity, "I am not unused to young girls. I have daughters, you know." That was true, but Davan knew that truth had no relevance to Teena.

Davan was not given to self-analysis, he believed he took each day as it came. If it was a day full of Teena, well, that was what office life was now—co-sexed. There was no need for him to reproach himself if he patted Teena's leg in sympathy, or loaned her money which she scarcely ever repaid. With a clean conscience, he went sedately home in the evening.

Falvey was in the habit of remarking sententiously that office life had everything in these hard times: "God help poor prostitutes, and as for servants and lower-class skivvies—begob, James Joyce ought to be alive and well and living in Dublin today! He could have his pick of the third-level beauties, in three languages as well!" Davan always replied coldly, "We didn't invent the system."

"Who bought the tie for you?" asked Teena, fingering the tie and smoothing his lapels.

He gave her his careful quarter-smile. Unlike his hair, his teeth were not his own.

"It's going to be awful here when you're gone!" She pouted rather attractively, "Falvey is pure torture!"

Softly, he patted her leg so conveniently placed against his hand. Thin legs, he thought vaguely, something about thin legs. She leaned a little closer. This was their unspoken game, so near and yet so far. Today, Teena was enthrallingly full of regrets.

"I'll miss you awful, Hugh. I wish you weren't leaving...who'll buy me a chocolate bikky for elevenses...who'll lend me a few bob on a Thursday? Do I still owe you from last week...I'm always forgetting...not to mention the ciggies you give me! That Falvey doesn't even smoke! Hey Hugh, what about your big glass ashtray? Can I have it?"

He slid the ashtray along the desk with his free hand. He could smell stale cigarette from her breath. It was intoxicating, intimate.

"You smoke too many cigarettes," he chided gently, fatherly, pressing home the message on her leg.

She tittered, "Too many old fags, too many sexy movies, too many late nights, too many chocolate bikkies...Who'll look after me when you're not here any more?" Her peaky face came closer, "I'm going to miss you awful," she whispered.

Through the glass panel, Davan saw Falvey's bulky shadow. He stood up swiftly and walked over to the window. Teena slipped off the desk, suddenly finding the *Times* of great interest.

"Am I interrupting anything?" bawled Falvey by way of greeting. "The Angel Gabriel and the Virgin Mary, by Picasso! Huh? You are not insensible to the compliment, Mary Christina, I hope?"

It was best to ignore Falvey. It was too late now to start teaching him manners. Teena sniffed loudly as if bursting with grief. Falvey began to sing:

Your father was laughing
Your mother was laughing
And I was laughing tooooooooooo
At last we got rid of you oo oo.

Davan permitted himself a wintry smile, "The laughter will be mutual, Falvey."

"Ah no hard feelings, Hugh! Don't get up on your high horse! Aren't you always saying yourself, 'Every dog has his day.' We'll all go sometime, even typists—even good typists—isn't that right, Mary Christina?"

"Mr Falvey, you're awful!" she spluttered.

"Tell you what," said Falvey, "here's something to keep your heart up…when the Great White God is gone, you may be allowed to call me Tom."

"And what will you call me then?" she asked pertly.

"Begob, you will always be Mary Christina to me to the end of your days! No baby talk for me—your Ma must have paid five bob to have you christened!"

Davan was still standing by the window. Through Falvey's loud-mouthed banter, he was remembering himself as a boy clerk in the ground-floor office. No girls in offices in those days. The day he joined the firm was the only day he had seen the owner-manager. From him, Davan had got the bare indoctrination considered enough: "We handle confidential business here, young lad. Don't mix our business and your private life. Remember that. And never piss on your own doorstep." Davan reflected wryly that no boss man would dare tell Falvey where not to piss. What would that long-dead boss make of Teena as a secretary in full possession of his confidential files?

Davan took the money from his pocket, and laid it on the table.

"I want everyone to have a couple of drinks before I go, Tom. Will you look after it?"

Falvey expanded his nostrils like a thirsty actor. He took the fivers, made lists and calculations, and hurried out to find a messenger. One of Teena's innumerable girl-friends was on the phone and Teena was listening to the latest gossip with strained attention. As Davan headed for the door, she blew him a kiss which he acknowledged with the usual guarded quarter-smile.

He left the building with the vague intention of going for a cup of coffee. He crossed the road, and went into the Green. He found a sheltered bench in the sunshine. A cat-nap would take care of the hour before the presentation. The dry thought flitted across his eyelids that his last hour was the only hour he had ever idled on the job.

The drinks went down well; the speeches were good-humoured and brief; the presentation was over. Hugh Davan had lodged the golden handshake in the bank, and with the excellent silver salver on the car-seat beside him, he was on his way home to lunch.

There were prickings of unaccustomed thoughts, even slight tendencies to emotion at the back of his mind—probably brought on by the quick drinks at midday. It was not his way to delve about in his psyche. He felt, instinctively, that delvers came up with things they could not handle. He took a peek at the sky and concentrated his thoughts on the first green. A little nap after lunch, he would be ready to tee-up as the afternoon golfers were going in, the ideal time to make a four. A few drinks afterwards in the club bar would give him a chance to expatiate on his handsome presentation and handshake. No harm in a small exaggeration, "handsome" was the word his club colleagues would like to hear.

In the entrance hall of his house were two suitcases. They looked new—no old air-stickers of the returned traveller. He walked into the kitchen.

"Have we a visitor? I didn't know we were expecting anyone?"

From the cooker, his wife glanced around at him.

"Oh," she said airily, "you are back. Lunch is just ready. Will you go ahead into the dining-room."

He stood his ground. His awareness was unaccountably heightened. It was not an ordinary morning, an enquiry from her was strangely missing.

"Who owns the suitcases?" he demanded.

"I do," she answered evenly.

The first green was still on his mind, but new suitcases in the hall were, to say the least, somewhat unusual. He hesitated.

"Would you prefer your lunch, or an explanation?" she asked most courteously.

He walked into the dining-room.

In a few minutes, she brought a tray. They began to eat in silence. She was a tip-top cook. It was a talent in her that he often thought of boasting about in the golf club, even to describing in detail excellent meals he had enjoyed at home. But then, he was not the boasting type.

"The office staff gave me a beautiful silver salver," he said, "a huge thing." His wife took a drink of water. "And of course," he added, "I got the usual bit of a golden handshake."

"That's nice," she said in the same even tone.

Davan felt a twinge of premonition. Years ago that precise, dry voice was the prelude to a tearing row: it signalled that she had been bottling-up grievances, and was about to explode in wrath. Like a shout in the Alps, one stray word from him would let loose an avalanche. If she once got launched, it could be goodbye to golf for today. He maintained an apprehensive silence, cheering himself with the thought that it was a long, long time since they had had a row. It had taken years but she had eventually learned her lesson. He prided himself on his ability to have himself well thought of by all his acquaintances; he felt that people respected him. He believed he had got that message across to his wife: that he was a popular, deservedly popular, figure in the world outside the home, and therefore he should be accorded the same consideration, and respect, within the home. He kept the roof over their heads and the bread in their mouths. When he was not at the club, he sat at home in front of the television. She always knew where he was, unlike a lot of men and their wives. For him, there had never been any extra-mural sex adventures. Oh, never. He had had his chances, plenty of them, but it all boils down to money. Money that had to be found for school fees and football boots, always something, and never enough. Yes, he had finally got it to her that he was a good man. No genius, mind you, an average chap, but good and worthy of her respect. And the rows had ceased, petered out, died a natural death. What had the rows been about, anyhow? Nothing! Absolutely nothing! He could not remember anything about them now except how fed up he used to get with her voice at three o'clock in the morning when all he could think of was that he had to get up at seven and face a day's work. Oh well, that was all years ago. Long experience warned him to keep his eyes on his plate, finish quietly, and take his apprehensive silence into the comfortable sitting-room there to plan the strategic moment of departure for the afternoon game.

"I am ready to speak to you about my suitcases," she walked through the glass doors into the sitting-room. She took her favourite position in her armchair beside the window. She liked to look out at the garden, and at the quiet road beyond the garden gate. Davan realised he had been dozing off. He glanced at his watch as she spoke:

"What I have to say won't take all day. I am leaving you. Today."

He stared at her. She looked much as usual, he supposed. Her hair was freshly groomed. Her face had not changed a great deal in all the years. If anything, her expression was more serene than he remembered. Serene and sort of smug. He noticed her new coat, and silk scarf.

"You are mad!" he half-shouted.

She had been looking at him, now she gazed calmly out of the window into the neat garden.

"What about the family?" he demanded.

"Family!" she repeated. "What is a family when they no longer live at home. Not even in Ireland. Father Paddy in the Philippines, Mary with three children in Canada, Con married and settled in England, and now Sheila and her Spanish husband teaching in California. They are all settled now. As you always said, you were a good provider. They don't need me even as an occasional baby-sitter." She smiled, quite at ease, and added, "Thank God."

The words in his throat choked each other. What about me? What about me? He knew at once that his pride would never allow him to plead for himself. His pride had always kept him incommunicado in the past when she started her antics. A man had to have his pride when his wife attacked him. Let her rip. She hadn't the gratitude of a louse. Never had. And today of all days...

"It had to be today," she said, reading his thoughts and speaking in that dry, even tone that he detested. "From tomorrow you will be moving in a new and different circle, your domestic circumstances unknown...no embarrassment...as for the golf club I never met..."

Her lips went on moving but he ceased to listen. She was confronting him with a planned betrayal. Sneaking up on him out of the blue, a planned bloody betrayal. And for what? The prim deliberate voice. All rehearsed. And what about the marriage vows? For better for worse until death do us part? How will her precious Father Paddy feel about that? A planned bloody betrayal. He began to feel very angry in a way he had never felt angry. He gripped his chair. It would be a pleasure to hit her.

"Do you expect me to make you an allowance because I won't," he shouted, "If you go out of this house, you are never..."

She interrupted him quickly, "I am never coming back. It is over." Her eyes were on his face. Her expression was neither cold nor warm, merely steady. A thought came to him, and he glared at her, "You have no claim on me, you understand? Neither on me nor on this house. Deserters are entitled to nothing. Nothing, you understand?"

She indicated an envelope on the window-sill, "I have written it down. I have no claim on you. I am pleasing myself. The cheque is for a considerable sum. I hope it will wipe out any claim *you* might have on me, it is my keep for thirty years, not excessively generous but in line with what it was..."

Did he detect a sneer in her voice when she said "excessively generous?" One of her gripes, he suddenly remembered, was that he was excessively mean. Forgotten sarcastic words came back to him vividly: that he treated every household bill as a major catastrophe, a broken cup was a calamity; that she was expected to weave clothes for herself and the children out of the morning mist. Oh yes, she was a great one for sarcasm when they were young, but that wasn't yesterday. No, and what was more, he, personally, was glad to forget all that. What had she to complain about now? What money was she talking about?

"Is it the few pounds your uncle was going to leave you?"

"It was quite a few!" she retorted lightly. "When

Sheila got married, and the money came through, my way was clear. I, too, had got my golden handshake."

A car had drawn up outside the front gate. Davan could see it was a taxi.

She rose unhurriedly, slowly gathering her handbag from a chair, pausing a moment at a mirror. Davan stared at her. There were no words.

The soft slam of the hall door echoed for only a second.

And Buttercups
All in a Row

May Grace loved her garden. Her family had come, they had grown up and gone their separate ways. They had, as it were, passed through her life. The garden had remained. Her husband, Terence, had passed through her life also but rather more importantly, his value to the garden was never forgotten.

"Trancie's idea it was to put down the beech hedges—the very first year. Look at them now and the age they are! Was there ever such a perfect shelter for flowers? Those columbine are tall as ballet dancers, yet they are protected perfectly from every breeze."

It seemed as if nothing had ever failed in Mrs Grace's garden. The most devastating winters wrought scarcely any damage. Sharp frosts in May did their bitter work elsewhere. Her long-dead Trancie received his regular accolade: "All due to the beech hedges...look at the height of the *penstemon* and the *monarda*, and the red brilliance of them...have you ever seen delphiniums so blue or so compact, or so many colours in lupins? All due to Trancie's beech! The shelter and the warmth!"

Trancie had built the low stone walls with local stone; he had designed the wrought-iron gates; he had constructed the summer-house with boughs from fallen trees.

"A great man with his hands for the stones and the grill-work but the beech hedges were the only growing thing he ever touched. He wouldn't know a paeony from a poppy! 'The red pompoms,' he used to say whether it was a rose or a dahlia!"

The truth was, of course, that the garden was the product of Mrs Grace's special genius, an acre of rough thistles transformed into a little Eden. Stone walls and iron gates are put together, finished, done with. A garden consumes a lifetime of loving. It takes the utter devotion of a lover to weed and dead-head and tie up and clip and snip and water and fertilise, day in day out, in all weathers. Manic devotion, but Mrs Grace did not quite admit that:

"It would be nearly idolatry if I didn't know that the best of my flowers always go to the four altars in the church," and she did not blink an eye when she said it. On Friday afternoons all through the year, in a spirit of joyful devotion and careful artistry she decked the altars. She was sure the congregation looked forward to seeing the church beautifully festooned on Sundays, and especially on feast-days.

On select occasions Mrs Grace could be persuaded to open the garden to little tours, and answer questions as to how the garden grew and prospered from its rough beginnings as an acre of thistle and gorse and rush never turned over in living memory until Trancie bought the site when he came as head-teacher to the local school. Fifteen pounds he paid for it, and that was a lot of money in those days. Trancie's idea it was to put in the beech hedges. It fascinated him that the beech never lost a leaf, only growing browner and drier, until all the brown was replaced by vivid green in springtime. The shelter was there all the time. The beech was the foundation of the garden's perennial beauty.

The garden was cunningly planned. There were divisions box-edged, all within the sheltering beeches. The beginning was full of old-fashioned flowers with old-fashioned names: rose campion, black-eyed susan, hostas, hemerocallis, phlox and many others all edged-about with the plush grey leaves of stachys. There were lattice fences supporting wistarias, tropaeolum, magnolia all in their season. Then there was a perfume garden in silvery, mauve and saffron shades, headily scented with lavender, bergamot, nicotiana, carnations and stock. There were raised beds of herbs and they were not just parsley and thyme; but also fennel, marjoram, tarragon—mainly grown for the joy of the unusual. The rose-garden was very spacious. There were always hundreds of roses: bushes, standards, climbers—a riot of red and gold in summertime. The rose-garden opened out into the real show-piece: curving lawns backed by massive herbaceous flowers of every type and description. The lawns themselves were like green carpets. The summer-house at the head of the garden, set to catch the evening sun, was covered in an ancient clematis of an apricot colour.

There was no doubt but that Mrs Grace knew all the secrets. Of course, she had shelves of gardening books which she studied continuously, adding hundreds of notes in the margins.

In latter years, the little garden tours always ended with someone's suggestion, "Do you know what it is, Mrs Grace—you should be on television—in full colour!"

Mrs Grace was all for television. It was a nice idea they had planted in her mind, like a tender pelargonium cutting that would surely send out roots, and promise a lovely flower. Cuttings, or ideas, the ripening of a root formation was the thing to wait for.

Wrapped in her cosy dressing-gown, Mrs Grace invariably took her first cup of tea out into the garden. Carrying the cup in one hand and the small secateurs in the other she set off from the kitchen door. The garden was her first thought on waking, her last long look at night from the bedroom window. This had been her routine since long ago when the garden first began to take shape. There had been hundreds of glorious mornings when she had run straight out in her nightie, flitting from flower to flower as light as a butterfly, blowing kisses to Trancie up at the bedroom window.

That was long ago. For many years, that was the nicest part of the day. Pride was uppermost and satisfaction. She could quickly assess what garden work would come later, what would be best to do that day. Contented, she would hurry indoors to do the mundane chores of attending to Trancie, and the family, and the house, in as quick a time as it took to be free for the real pleasure-work.

A time came when there was no one to untidy the house, only one bed to make, one small appetite to cater for. Now she had entered on the happiest time of all. There was never a hint of loneliness. She fully comprehended that a garden will accept every lavishment and in return will fulfil every need. If the occasional twinge of stiffness in the joints brought fear of rheumatism (and a garden gone to seed), May Grace banished the fear. That time had not come yet.

Until the sunny morning she rounded the gable-end of the house to see a long black shadow across the front lawn. Setting down the cup and the secateurs, she peered into the dense leaves to see why the sun was not twinkling through her beech hedge. The light was blocked by something as big as a railway-carriage.

Nervously clutching the lapels of her dressing-gown, Mrs Grace unlatched the big wooden gate. She peeped out. There was a very big transport van parked alongside her hedge. It was painted in shining black. The sides and back were emblazoned in red:

FREDDY'S FAST FOOD.

She slammed the gate quickly. She had a sense of unaccustomed shock. There had never been a stranger's car, much less a huge lorry, parked outside her gate, nor indeed on her road. It was a very narrow winding boreen that had once been part of the old country road, cut off and discontinued many years ago. The main highway now lay a quarter-mile away, the traffic inaudible. Away up at the top of her old road was the church, now approached from the highway; and beyond the church the little town. At the other end, and on the highway, were the new football fields.

Mrs Grace sat at the kitchen table, sadly debating the possibility of a beleaguered position on a disused byway where huge articulated trucks could park overnight, maybe with their drivers inside them, maybe foreigners? Or maybe, a more dreadful thought, a byway where shady characters could park their old cars and leave them to rot. What was called, she had heard, a "car-graveyard."

Sensibly dressed, and business-like, she went out to the front gate. After all, the obvious thing to do was to request Freddy (whoever he might be) to shift himself. Move off! Park somewhere else!

There was no one in the lorry. She tapped on the sides, and called out with forced politeness, "Mr Freddy!" She walked around the vehicle. It was quite splendidly new. On one side it was hinged, she observed. It was easy to visualise a flap lifted, and a shop revealed within.

She would ring the guards. The guards would help her—that was their job. The sergeant's wife had brought her own visiting relatives to see the garden several times, and had always been given a bouquet on leaving.

"Oh is that you, Sergeant Mulloy? This is Mrs Grace. Mrs Grace...yes, Sergeant, Mrs Grace of the garden...the garden, yes, well I have a problem..."

Sergeant Mulloy wanted to ask Mrs Grace "how does your garden grow?" He had a weakness for rhymes and riddles, and he had often tried that one on the schoolchildren:

> "Mary, Mary, quite contrary
> How does your garden grow?
> Silver bells and cockle shells
> And buttercups all in a row."

He usually had to get to the last line before they chimed in. It seemed a pity not to use his old rhyme to make a bit of fun, but he composed himself to listen as the poor lady launched into a tale of woe.

She was describing her feelings of shock at what

she called an invasion, rushing on into forebodings of the ghastly acts of rascals who set up car-graveyards, and the fears of a lone woman in proximity to overnight long-distance lorry drivers—maybe foreigners without a civil word of English. And, in the wake of that, maybe week-ending caravans looking for toilet facilities; or even worse, itinerants' ramshackle settlements and their washing hung on her beech hedges...

The sergeant, a kindly enough man left to himself, let the old lady run on. They all get winded eventually.

"Freddy did you say?" queried the sergeant, plunging into a pause for breath. "Freddy? There's no Freddies around here. Wait a minute now...he must be over from Glenbeg. I heard tell two of the families over there went into the trucking business lately—they sold a couple of small farms to that fellow has the big stud farm. I can't think of his name for the life of me, but he bought a lot of land lately...Was it Harrison or...?"

"And you will come over, Sergeant, and move them on? You will, won't you, straightaway?"

"Ah well now, Mrs Grace, I wouldn't like to raise your hopes. You see, M'am, there's no yellow lines on that old road, and, providing (providing, mind you) that Freddy has paid his road tax, he can park there with impunity...with impunity—." The sergeant relished round phrases of that sort, they were reassuring, they had the ring of legality "—with impunity, M'am, for as long as he likes. After all, Freddy is not impeding anybody."

Mrs Grace went out to the garden for comfort and consolation. She averted her eyes from the black bulk beyond the hedge. There were tasks waiting for her to do today as on all her days from time immemorial. Today her thumbs were aching, her knees were stiff, her eyes were full of tears. She sat in Trancie's summer-house, barely able to think.

Bereft of all spirit is she who cannot fight back. By the next day, May Grace had decided to say no more to the guards. She would put the matter in the hands of a solicitor, and put her trust in God. God looks after the widow and the orphan. It might be a good idea to approach God through the parish priest...unless all his powers were limited by statutory regulations, like the guards.

As it happened, on Friday when she took her flowers to decorate the altars for Sunday, the parish priest was putting up notices in the church. He fussed over her as she set out her blooms and greenery on a table.

"Big special efforts this week, eh, Mrs Grace? Many strange faces at masses this Sunday! And next Sunday too, by the help of God! Big impression! Hum? Hum?"

"Father, I was going to ask you..." but he did not seem to hear her. He took more notices from a cupboard, he held them up for her to admire them, "I got these printed by the *Democrat*. They were dear enough, God knows, only half the price a few years ago. But the committee will reimburse me. Nice way they set it out. Very clear, no mistakes."

As Mrs Grace stood up, she glimpsed the words in vivid green: Programme, Festival.

"Father," she said in a loud voice, "perhaps you could spare a moment. I am upset..." the word "upset" was lost in the priest's voluble exclamation,

"Oh Oh deary me—look at the time. I promised Father Keogh to let him have these posters over in the school for the parents' meeting this evening. All hands to the wheel, you know, for a big fund-raising project like the festival! I held out against a festival in other years, you know, but now we are landed into one, I do believe it will be an outstanding success. Would you believe, we have sold over four hundred tickets for the teenagers' disco in the hall? And the raffle-tickets are going marvellously well. Of course, the prizes are good: a holiday for two in Tramore, and as for the whiskey, and wine—I must say the publicans in the parish were more than generous. And the Rolex watch! I do hope the right person wins. I myself have bought a number of tickets. It is a beauty...solid gold, you know. And you won't be lonely, Mrs Grace. A lot of the action will go on in the new sports complex over beyond your place. And on your side of the church down a bit of the old road, we will have the big marquee for the traditional music, and the Irish dancing competitions..."

He continued his enthusiastic if one-sided communication, making his way out of the church. Mrs Grace never had a chance to get a word in. Her first instinct was to gather up her flowers and go home...to be revenged. But on what? She would do St Anne's altar and no more. She had an old affection for St Anne's little altar. The statue of St Anne carried a sheaf of flowers on which the saint's downcast eyes bestowed interest. May Grace always felt a reciprocal interest in dressing this little altar with special whites and greens.

In the end, she decorated all the altars. Today she

was slow. The customary bustle of her movements seemed to have deserted her. She usually sat down at last to rest, to say a decade of the rosary, and to gaze (justifiably proud) at the results of her work. Today she did not pause. She was anxious to be gone. She did not read the parish priest's posters. Their myriad implications were printed on her mind.

Later in the day, there was noise of activity on the road accompanied by a blaring radio. Very soon, there was a loud knocking on the big wooden gate which Mrs Grace now kept locked.

A slim young woman, dressed in jeans and a sun-top, was standing on the road. Before an angry Mrs Grace could speak to protest about the noise, the young woman exclaimed excitedly,

"What a lovely garden you've got!"

Slightly mollified, Mrs Grace reduced the key of her expostulation.

"I am afraid I must ask..."

"Oh will you look at those roses! And the heavenly scent! Dicky! Dicky! Come and see the garden!"

Another pretty young woman appeared out of the big black van. Her jeans had been scissored-off well above the knee, and her long black hair swung about like a pony's tail.

"This is my sister, Deirdre. You're Mrs Grace, aren't you?"

Mrs Grace felt it was time to take a firm stand.

"I would like to speak to your father, Miss, if you please."

"Our father?" The girl looked puzzled.

"Mr, uh Mr, er Freddy," said Mrs Grace, the

determination drained out of her, confronted by their youthful liveliness. They were smiling broadly.

"I am Freddy," the first girl said, "and this is our van. Father Haloran told us to park here so we would be near water. He told us you were devoted to the church, and we could depend on you for the water. OK? Isn't that what he said, Dicky?"

"Yeh! On account of the festival being for parish funds. It's the roof, or the new organ-loft."

"No," her sister said, "the last one over in Knockatore was for the organ-loft, this one is for the new roof. Father Haloran told us you were the most obliging lady in the parish!"

Mrs Grace found it hard to respond. She was certain that in a village with no public water supply, the parish priest's plumbing was better equipped to supply extra water than her small well was. The garden needed a lot, and in this long dry summer the rain-barrels were low.

"Do you need much water?" she asked.

"Oceans!" replied Miss Dicky, "We don't have much demand for tea or coffee, but the washing-up is endless after chips and beans and burgers and sausages. The kids drink minerals mostly but you know kids, they would eat chips all night!"

Full of misgiving, Mrs Grace supplied the water, many buckets of it, which they stored into a tank in the van.

"The kids will all be over tonight," Miss Dicky chatted as she trotted in and out with the buckets, "you know kids! They go mad on the first night. The festival really only starts with high mass at eleven tomorrow morning, but you know kids—they never wait. I heard there will be about a hundred on their old bangers over from Ballybeg—they all got the bangers when the factory started. They're mad, those kids!"

"Bangers?" queried Mrs Grace faintly.

"Old beat-up motor-bikes, souped-up, you know!"

Mrs Grace was puzzled, "Kids on motor-bikes?"

Miss Dicky laughed, "Well, the kids would be the teens into twenties—like us, kinda."

Miss Freddy pretended wrath, "Speak for yourself, kiddo!"

Even when Mrs Grace went into her kitchen, the noise of the transistor followed her and even when she pressed in the clasps on all the windows shutting out the perfume of her roses, it was still there disturbing her thoughts. Her resentment against the parked truck had been given a twist when she found that Freddy was a woman. And a likeable woman, polite, attractive, hard-working. Mrs Grace needed to talk, she needed to sort out her confusion, to pour out her troubles into a friendly ear. She phoned her elder daughter, Mary. It was not, Mary told her, a suitable evening for a heart-to-heart. Mary had dinner guests, arriving at seven-thirty...very important guests...most things were ready...but there was still her shower...and last-minute touches...she was sure her mother understood. Mrs Grace understood that Mary knew only very important people, nevertheless she needed to be heard and she persisted.

"Mother, I do believe you are going to cry! For heaven's sake, listen to me...I expect it will only be for a week. These village festivals always peter out after the first couple of days. Don't be silly, of course your road won't be occupied by every dog and devil! Such a thing to say! Ah now Mam, stop going on...wait, I've got a good idea! No, listen, I'll get the children to pray for rain—that'll put a damper on the sausage and chip idea! What? What did you say? Well, who would walk down that road ploughed up with muck? Oh yes it would. I remember it in the winter when I was a kid coming from school. Rain is the answer to all your problems, Mam! We'll all pray! What? Oh no, the children won't mind if it rains—we are off to Spain on Tuesday. Yes, Mam, I did tell you it was this Tuesday. No, Mam, this Tuesday, so I won't be able to come out to see you...and, Mam, listen, I just have to break off here...I must nip out to the kitchen, it is one of my special menus. Now cheer up, Mam, you cannot expect the world to revolve around your garden."

Mrs Grace dropped the receiver. There was not much use ringing Liz in Canada. Liz might be more sympathetic than Mary, but she was far away and Mrs Grace could never remember what time of the clock it might be in Canada, probably the middle of the night. Tom and Frank? Their wives decided for them the time of the year they could visit their mother, certainly not on an impulsive phone-call. What could they do, anyway? They did not even have children to pray for rain.

She had lost interest in cooking her evening meal. Automatically she went out into the garden. Now the smell of boiling oil was everywhere, oil boiling for the chips, oil boiling to the raucous rhythm of the incessant radio.

There was no sleep for Mrs Grace that night. The ear-splitting vibrations of revving motor-bikes and car-horns were added to a screeching mixture of voices above the ever louder radio, or tape-recorder, or whatever guaranteed the endless jangle.

At dawn, Mrs Grace went into the garden. She stood and stared. There were papers and cans thrown over the hedge and stuffed into the hedge. The unsightly scene suggested that hundreds of people must have gorged themselves on Freddy's Fast Food, and regurgitated it over her wooden gate. She brought buckets of water to sluice away the sour-smelling mess. It took longer to fill refuse sacks with the gluey papers, and sticky cans, and rubbish which had to be lifted with a garden trowel, so noisome was it. Her back was aching when at last she could attend to the flower beds.

She gave the sergeant time to have his breakfast and then she phoned him. She complained in the strongest possible terms.

It seemed a bit odd to threaten the law on the sergeant of the guards. Having done so, however, she rang the local solicitor and put him in full possession of the facts. He was courteous, but discreetly full of caution.

"I should like very much to help you, Mrs Grace. Indeed, you have my utmost sympathy. All you have told me is sad, very sad. Indeed an injunction under the circumstances might be considered. However, the transitory nature of the transgression presents a difficulty. Now, Mrs Grace, it would help me enormously if you would set down all the circumstances in the form of a letter, adding such details as your age, your widowhood, your living alone, and of course your great interest in gardening..."

There would be peace now until the evening revels began again. May sat in Trancie's summer-house, idle and dreaming of the old days long ago. The garden had been a magnificent background for the pictures of the girls' wedding days. And much further back for the First Communion days. The little girls in their dainty veils against the roses; the boys, in their first blazers posed, manly-like, by Trancie's elegant iron gates. Those were happy times in the garden, and she had not taken time to think of them. Ah she was too busy. Through half-closed eyes she pictured the lawn peopled with family and friends, the while she wondered vaguely at herself for sitting when there was always so much to do.

In the afternoon, the sergeant came.

"Well now, Mrs Grace, fine and well you are looking! And is this the garden that the missus is always talking about? Sure you keep it gorgeous! Every bud in place and silver bells and the lot! And they tell me you do it all yourself? Ah sure it's no bother to you and you with all day to do it, but I admit I never saw better…"

He had a list of easy compliments as long as his arm. He could go on all night and no amount of Mrs Grace's interruptions about how dreadful the garden had looked this morning, or about the possible shortage of water, ever got beyond a few syllables. He spent the first litany of fulsome clichés edging himself into the garden, and the second litany of ancient saws edging himself out.

"Ah sure, boys will be boys, Mrs Grace, and we can't put old heads on young shoulders. Out diverting themselves as only the youth can! What did the poet say about the 'days of our glory'…was it in Moore's *Melodies*, huh? Ah sure weren't we young ourselves...Love's Young Dream...dressing themselves up and eating chips all night. No harm in them at all. All glitter like the first star in the sky and no thought for tomorrow..."

Nor for other people's property either, thought Mrs Grace as she locked the wooden gate. And they can go hang for their water.

But of course she gave them the water. She passed another sleepless night. She spent another morning cleaning up the filth. And another. And another.

The weather held good, there was no rain. On Thursday the well was dry, the electric pump brought up no more than a few drops. She informed the girls.

"Not to worry!" Miss Dicky said cheerfully, "Father Haloran is sending over one of those big bulk water carriers. We will park it here beside us, it will do us for the rest of the week. It'll be handier than dragging the buckets in and out...so don't give it another thought! Freddy says Saturday will be murder and mayhem so buy your ear-plugs, Mrs Grace!"

On Friday morning, Mrs Grace did not feel able to get up. She thought dimly of her usual morning cup of tea. The long-life milk was finished out, and she had done no Thursday shopping. Today she would have to prepare her blooms for the altars. Still she did not rise because she knew she would have to steel herself for the first look from the bedroom window into her beloved garden. The shock had not lessened with the passing days. Each morning, the desecration was worse. The pain of it gripped her heart. Maybe later in the day, she would get up the courage. Maybe later in the day, she would continue the letter to Liz or perhaps begin a new one—not so sad, not so full of moans. Liz was always the soft-hearted one. Maybe later in the day, she would find the strength to get up and cook a little meal for herself...she could not remember when she had eaten. Maybe later in the day, she would use the water in the rain-barrels for some of her most precious plants. Maybe...just now it seemed easier to drift off to sleep.

From Father Haloran right down to the poorest church mouse, the festival was accounted an enormous triumph, financially and every other way. Now the church could get a new roof. Indeed, at the Sunday mass, Father hinted at great innovations for the benefit of the parish. The Irish dancing competitions and the competitions for traditional Irish music, Father Haloran went on, were overwhelmingly successful. It was like times long ago, before cinemas and discos, when the jigs and reels were danced at the local cross-roads. To wind up the festival, all the dancers and musicians had stepped-it-out all night down on the old road—danced the night away, you might say, under the moon—and, Father Haloran liked a touch of humour, no doubt they were sustained by the fast food available! A television camera had them all on film, he added, so they would have the pleasure of seeing the whole parish on the "box" next week.

The television crew, high up on their gantry to film the jigs and reels of the night-long ceilidhe, had spotted the garden behind the high beech hedges. In a village totally lacking in scenic appeal, the lovely, colourful garden was a stroke of luck. It would furnish out the Festival Film with a distinctive difference. On the Monday morning, they came back to get the owner's permission to commence the filming. They would film her, too, and give her the chance to say a few proud words. They had enquired, and found that indeed she was very proud of her glorious garden. They were ready to tell her that the garden would be on video in full magnificent technicolour.

The road was empty now of everything but the County Council refuse lorry, and a few men who were cleaning the litter. The television crew got no answer to their repeated bangings on the wooden gates. One of them shinned over a wall at the back of the house. He tried the bell and the knocker on the front door. There was no response. Eventually he opened the wooden gates and joined his mates outside. One of them had noticed that there was a light in an upstairs room.

Mrs Grace's body was taken away for the post-mortem. The village never learned the actual cause of death, or maybe they preferred the mystery of it. In due course, the family brought back Mrs Grace's remains for interment side by side with her husband Terence and almost within call of his beech hedges.

The congregation straggled out of the graveyard on to the village street, and the sergeant had the last word: "Comes like a thief in the night and sure no one knows the day nor the hour; it's you today and me tomorrow; the clock strikes the march of time and who can put a stop to progress?"

No one mentioned the garden.

The Adultery

The woman opened her eyes reluctantly. The young priest had come again. He was drawing the chair to her bedside, he was seating himself, he was taking out a notebook. Surely he knew her name by now? This must be his third visit, or maybe his fourth. She knew she had lost count of the days. It was no matter, sufficient for her to endure the timelessness without trying to keep track of it.

The priest had found her name in his notebook. He pencilled a small mark beside it. Was it a neat tick, or a question mark?

"Good morning, Mrs Gray."

Ah, it was a question mark after all. His eyes were bright with interrogation. An ever-present weariness intensified its hold in her head. Not to drift into the dimness beyond the bed was an immense effort. Sheer courtesy compelled her to focus her eyes on the earnest face of the young priest.

"Good morning, Father," she whispered.

"Ah, that's better!" he said vigorously as if his very briskness could infuse life into her. "Sister tells me you had a good night last night, plenty of rest?"

Much Sister knows about it, Eily Gray thought.

"And able to eat some nice breakfast, too,"

continued the young priest in the same hearty, coaxing tone.

"Some tea," she responded faintly. And revolting it tasted, dusty and cold.

"Nothing like a nice cup of tea," the young priest beamed.

Sister had told him there was not much time left, and not to waste it with preliminary talk. The hospital sister was a force to be reckoned with in his work. Each sister was a deeply religious and utterly devoted nun. No one was allowed to forget that. The sick body, regrettably, could not always be renewed and made good; the soul could, and must. His own vocation seconded that, profoundly. In the face of this woman's ebbing strength, the haste of the task had proved daunting.

"I prayed for you in my mass this morning, Mrs Gray."

"What kind of prayer?" He could see that she was touched. From her earliest years, she would have known that to be remembered in a priest's mass was a great honour. He smiled to take the edge off his words, "A prayer for grace to melt the stubborn heart."

Her thoughts came together only to fly astray in all directions. With difficulty she marshalled them and tried to direct them at the priest. "I do not wish to make a confession, not now. I do not have any sins." That was silly, everyone had sins. She began again, struggling to clear her voice, "I did go to confession once, a long time ago. It was at Easter…it was not a good confession…" her voice faded and came back almost inaudibly…"I did penance. For twenty years, I did penance for something I don't believe in."

"It is twenty years, then, since your last confession?"

The woman looked at him. His voice was lowered to an almost-forgotten hush. He was trying to trap her by re-creating the sacramental intimacy of the confessional box. She did not speak. He persisted, "Does that mean you did not approach the altar of the Eucharist? In twenty years, you did not receive Holy Communion?"

Yes, it meant that. She barely nodded.

"Yet Sister tells me your husband is a daily communicant. He always goes to the evening mass here after visiting hour. The nuns have been much edified by his demeanour."

Ah, yes. Tom. But, of course. Low as her voice was, he was struck by the note of gentle sarcasm in it when she agreed that Tom was a saint, no one could doubt it. She was inclined to forget about Tom, now, here. Even when he arrived for the visiting hour, she could not quite place him. Was he her elder son, or perhaps he was her father-in-law? She had been very fond of Tom's father. There was an animal warmth about the man, very welcome to her nature. He was a big, rumpled man given to fierce bear-hugs, and prolonged hand-clasps. She thought, with an inward smile, of his rapturous welcomes and near-amorous farewells. Tom was almost as old now as his father had been when he died. He looked like his father now that he was ageing. He was never rumpled, of course, and his finger-tip greeting was frost-cold. Even his lips on her forehead were set and grim. All the same, maybe his lack of ardour made him the faithful kind. He was that, and a good provider.

She remembered her mother's saying, that a good provider was the first ingredient in a happy home. She fastened her thoughts on the aim of remembering to greet Tom kindly when he came to see her in the visiting hour. He was, after all, undemanding. He would perch there with his *Irish Times* open, ready to beguile the hour with a reading from the Deaths column, remarking always how many old friends and acquaintances were beginning to pass away these days.

She had lost the gist of the young priest's discourse, barely catching a word here and there about the mercy of Christ for sinners, the need for sanctifying grace, the everlasting glory of the immortal soul. She forced her eyes from their inward gaze onto his earnest face…"I see, of course, how innocent and tranquil your life has been. It would be simple to bless you and cease to trouble you, and equally simple for you, Mrs Gray, to go through the form, to recite a truly contrite act of contrition, and allow me, thereby, to give you a solemn absolution. Just reflect for a moment how simple it would be and how good you would feel afterwards."

She lifted her hand in a helpless gesture. "Yes, I know," he continued firmly, "that you admit to no serious sin since your last confession. And perhaps, even then, there were none. But maybe in the whole of your life there was an unconfessed—a forgotten sin—that could now be mentioned."

How very earnest he is, she mused. The letter of the law must be fulfilled. He would go away happy, her name ticked off in his notebook, her card stamped for heaven. How very earnest. If not successful today, he would be back tomorrow, and tomorrow, until all her tomorrows were gone.

"I should like to die in peace," she whispered. If there was a plea, the young priest failed to accede to it. He brightened visibly. "And so you shall!" he said. From an inner pocket, he took the small confessional stole, he pressed his lips to it and placed it about his shoulders.

"Bless yourself now," he said to the woman, and taking her hands in his, he helped her, "and repeat with me 'Bless me, Father, for I have sinned.'" She repeated the words with resignation, but slowly, unwillingly.

He encouraged her gently. "And now accuse yourself." Painfully, she drew a long breath. With her eyes on his, she brought out the sin for his inspection, "Adultery, Father."

It seemed to be good enough, or bad enough; his hands on hers relaxed away, and clasped in prayer, "You have not confessed this sin before? Tell me then."

The name of the sin was never enough, there had to be details. What details? It was so long ago, so brief, so unexpected. And yet it had weighed, unexpiated. Because if not confessed, then not forgiven, then not washed away in the waters of penance.

And why not confessed in that confessional all those years ago? Because it was the cherished secret. The secret, weighing on heart and conscience, had set at naught the tenets of her faith. The secret would not be bartered for peace of mind, it had become the substance of a bad confession. Was there a greater bad than that bad, a black lie before Christ in the person of his priest? More than that, and more grave than that, the precious secret had replaced all other belief.

"Maybe you could clear your throat a little," the young priest was saying, "here is some water. That's right, sip it slowly, slowly."

He is prepared to take all day at it now that he has a hold on me, she thought, and his prompting advice is getting mixed up with what I am trying to say. But no, he is only helping me, it is his duty.

"Well," she began softly but with a semblance of great determination, "it was during that time they called 'the Emergency' when Tom and all his friends joined the Irish army." She paused to draw a long, painful breath, "Were you even born then, Father, so long ago? Were we expecting a German invasion?"

Suddenly she remembered how handsome they had looked in their officers' uniforms. When Tom came home from barracks on short leaves, he always brought a few other fellows with him—lads whose families lived further away than we did. Those were great times when the house was crowded, it was lonely in between with only the children for company.

She had made a start, the words came stumbling out, confused and almost inaudible. The priest placed his watch on the bedside table. He had observed Sister pausing at the open door. Well, if he had to practise patience, so must she.

"...there were apple trees and lilac trees in the garden around the cottage, the cottage was our first home, Father..."

They took their meals into the garden. There was never enough food for more than a picnic. One of the lads had a mouth-organ. He could play anything. The children loved to run about to the music. The music was like happiness falling out of the trees, making them all light-hearted, and light-headed. Every moment in their lives, their constant separation, their dismal food rationing, the frightening daily news bulletins, made them all aware that the world was at war. Their joy in life was intensified, heightened, set free of all taboo. Their garden was the Garden of Eden under sunlight and moonlight, under skies so open that death and danger were only real very far away.

In between the great times, there were the lonely times for a young woman with two small children. It came about, tacitly, that if Tom would not be home, then one or other of the lads would try to break the monotony of Eily's week. Tom took it for granted that the lads were all very concerned for Eily. He seldom remembered to ask which of them turned up.

Eily became aware that the young priest had bent closer. She smiled as good a smile as she could manage. He was anxious that she should make a good confession, and she was mumbling away about a past that was as far away as the day she had made her very first confession...First Confession and the loving seriousness of everyone in the family instructing her, then!

"How many times will I say I told lies?" she asked, for the hundredth time. Eddie, her eldest brother, sat down on the stairs where she had waylaid him with this fearful problem.

"You don't tell lies," he told her, "they are only fibs! Silly fibs too—sure Mammy knows you're only making it up as you go along. She doesn't mind!"

"Oh but what about the priest? He doesn't know. If I say I told lies, he will say how many? And I always forget. If I say ten, maybe it was twenty—and that will be another lie."

"Look at you," he teased, "you're nearly crying! They are only fibs—ten or twenty, what's the difference?" He put his arm around her, hugging her, "Look, this is what you'll do...say, 'no more than fifty, Father.' Then you will be on the safe side!"

Her beloved brother, Eddie. He had gone off to that war she had been thinking about. So many girls had loved Eddie. Elusive handsome Eddie, was he ever afraid of confession or of anything? He had been killed in that war. Right at the end, when it was nearly over.

"Mrs Gray, you were saying that in the absence of your husband, you sought to attract one of his friends?"

She supposed that was what she had been saying. Accusing herself? Being on the safe side? Take away the loneliness, and the lack of money, and all the worry about the children not getting enough to eat...yes, she did start looking for attention.

The binding importance of being married to Tom had been forgotten. She had forgotten that...binding forever. For life, and beyond. The sacrament of matrimony. She had entered that state, a child out of school, and in those early years she was a child in marriage, child-wife, child-mother. It was like a game of house.

The young priest had to strain his ears. He felt she was making excuses in advance for what she was struggling to confess, if she ever got to it. He was a little impatient.

"Yes, yes," he said, "You were young. Myself, I see great good in our marriage guidance courses. No such thing when you were starting out, of course. Do you remember this particular young man's name, his first name?"

The moment he asked the question, the name flew away out of her mind. Memory had become like that as she became older. Memory chose the moment, and would not have strange fingers probing among its records. But she remembered the young man's face and his voice. She could hear the lilting southern tone of his voice telling her two little boys outrageous bedtime stories about a bumble bee called Barney. This famous bee kept a shop, full of jars of delicious honey, and he kept a school of bold drones and a racing stable. Barney drove a winged chariot and four borses (borses were bee-horses) all over Bumb Town. This small vulgarity always sent the children into fits of giggles.

"You are only encouraging them," she pleaded, "now they will never go to sleep."

He had a way with them, and they did snuggle down after a while. Then he and she went out to the garden to talk and talk and talk. He was a person who had much to share. He had read so many books she had never even heard of. And music. She had not known that music, without words, could interpret her thoughts and fill the landscape of her mind. He brought his records, "Close your eyes and listen, and I will too. Afterwards, we will tell each other what we saw."

It was a fascinating game. She unfolded to him innocently, sensuously, deep in the exploration of abstract beauty. Not for a moment did she so much as think of Tom when she entered this new world. When Tom came home, she returned to earth.

"Tom was as undemanding then as always since," she told the priest. "His gentle love-making at routine intervals was familiar, and accepted without question. That was how my life was in those years."

"Shall we walk up to the top of the hill tonight?" she asked the young man. "There's a gorgeous moon, and I know a place where we can look down into the valley and see all the peaks of the Wicklow mountains."

The neighbour was brought in to look after the sleeping children. The night was as mild as the day had been in the garden. Hand in hand, they left the road and took the path up the hillside. A silence, more intimate than their usual sharing, held them. They sat on a grassy hillock near the top, still holding hands, drawing warmth from their nearness...

The young priest waited, nursing his patience. It was evident her strength was failing, it was scarcely fair to ask her to continue.

Her eyes, asking for help, found his.

"You are coming to the end, Mrs Gray. Will I help you with your act of contrition?" But her eyes changed, flickering with rebellion. Her mind protested, there was no headlong passion of a moonlit night. Within me, there was a coming-of-age.

"We had never broken any rules, any barriers, not consciously..." Her voice faded, and then she found strength. Until that night, until that moment when he put his arms about her, and the grass came up behind their heads like a pillow, until then her feelings were all on the surface. Delight in him was uppermost, joy in his presence, enthusiasm for his enthusiasm. Now a rip-tide of emotion never before experienced swept her thoughts away. His voice was passionate, close to her face. She used to wish, in after years, that he had said he loved her. Maybe he did say that. Maybe he asked her to go away with him for ever. Implored her, perhaps? Maybe in that few moments of ecstasy there was a future for them in his mind. In her there was a shattering generosity of her body, an insatiable longing to give. Desire choked her voice, new-born love was there ready to be told...

"My hands were uncontrollable, tearing at his coat, and his hands were helping mine, while his words flew around my head. Somehow I knew what I was doing, Father, I knew a mortal sin would be committed. I did not care, I longed for it, I wanted it..." There was a long pause while the sick woman fought for breath..."That way of desire was not revealed to me in my marriage...not at that time...and not since..."

It seemed to the young priest that the faltering words had stopped for ever. He joined her hands in his. Slowly and distinctly, he said the act of contrition. She was still aware of him, he thought. It seemed as if her lips were forming the words.

The moon came from behind a cloud. And suddenly the man had pulled away. His movements were swift, almost rough, as he lifted her onto her feet, smoothing her dress, belting his coat. She wanted to protest, he silenced her by touching his fingers to her lips. He took her arm firmly to guide her back to the path, there he walked in front of her until they were on the road. Even then he did not speak, and pride kept her silent. She knew she was the one who had taken the initiative, and she had been rebuffed. She, who thought she knew his innermost depth, had not the slightest inkling of his feeling now. She saw him clearly as she walked beside him...he was an innocent man, she was a sinner.

The lovely months of slow retreat from her marriage had surely placed her in the path of seduction. She knew then, and forever, that seduction had taken place. It had taken place in her will and it had rooted in her soul.

Wearily, she opened her eyes. She was unsure if it was the young man, or the young priest, who was walking away from her. The priest would be back tomorrow if he was not satisfied with today. The young man she had never seen again, and now she could not remember his name.

In the evening, Tom came for the visiting hour. Sitting there with his *Irish Times*, she guessed he was seeking about in his mind for some nice thing to say. She knew he was abashed by her increasing frailty.

"Tell me about the weather, Tom," she whispered, a tiny thread of mischief in her voice.

"You're getting better now—you're getting cheeky!" They both knew she would not be getting better. She put her hand over his. His hand was cold, and did not know how to respond. She had pity for him.

"I never did enough for you, Tom." His eyes seemed to register surprise. He took his hand away. Quickly he took out a handkerchief and blew his nose. "You gave me a great life, girl."

Eily's determination to say some special word weakened. Her eyes would refuse to face his embarrassment even if her drifting senses could now lay hold on the tender love-words so long withheld. She could not remember why her throat was worn dry. And yet, some earlier time today, there was an unravelling of many tender words. It was like the falling of rose-petals at the exact moment the rose was ready. The petals, but never the secret of the rose. The secret was untouchable, and best left so.

"You are smiling," Tom said, "why are you smiling?"